SUPERDREADNOUGHT 3

SUPERDREADNOUGHT 3

SUPERDREADNOUGHT™ BOOK THREE

CH GIDEON CRAIG MARTELLE TIM MARQUITZ

MICHAEL ANDERLE

DISRUPTIVE IMAGINATION®

We can't write without those who support us
On the home front, we thank you for being there for us

We wouldn't be able to do this for a living if it weren't for our readers
We thank you for reading our books

CONNECT WITH THE AUTHORS

Craig Martelle Social

Website & Newsletter:
http://www.craigmartelle.com

Facebook:
https://www.facebook.com/AuthorCraigMartelle/

Michael Anderle Social

Website: http://www.lmbpn.com

Email List: https://lmbpn.com/email/
Facebook:
https://www.facebook.com/TheKurtherianGambitBooks/

SUPERDREADNOUGHT 3 TEAM

Thanks to our Beta Readers

James Caplan
Kelly O'Donnell
Micky Cocker
John Ashmore

Thanks to the JIT Readers

James Caplan
Kelly O'Donnell
John Ashmore
Jackey Hankard-Brodie
Mary Morris
Diane L. Smith
Peter Manis
Micky Cocker

If I've missed anyone, please let me know!

Editor
Lynne Stiegler

CHAPTER ONE

The SD *Reynolds* exited the Gate near the aquatic planet of Krokus 4…

Right into the middle of a battle.

"Oops!" Ensign Tanirika "Ria" Alcott muttered under her breath.

Alarms wailed, and the bridge was bathed in an unsettling wash of red lights. Bursts of cannon fire rattled the hull from both sides as the ship oriented itself.

"I'm starting to think you guys like seeing me get shot to fuck-all," Reynolds complained as what had happened began to register. "Deploy gravitic shields and report!"

"I'd say 'oops' fucking well covers it," Tactical stated.

"A little more detail would be nice," Reynolds grumbled.

Jiya Lemaire, First Officer, came over to stand alongside Reynolds' android form. She gripped the side of his seat to steady herself since the ship rocked with each blast.

"We're looking at two distinct entities," she told him. "There's a planetary force in a defensive posture, the larger destroyers there to our port, and the smaller attack array to our starboard—the red and black colored ships."

"Who's shooting holes in my ass?" Reynolds asked.

"Currently…both of them," Jiya replied, looking abashed.

The ship rumbled as blows crashed into the raised shields. Reynolds waved the alarms to silence, and the flashing red lights returned to normal.

"Both? What the fuck?"

"Well, we did kind of pop into the middle of their war," Jiya explained. "Can't really blame them."

"Oh, I can blame them plenty," Reynolds remarked. "Get us up and out of the crossfire."

"Already on it, sir," Ensign Alcott told him.

The blows to the ship began to subside seconds after she spoke. The viewscreen stopped flickering.

"We're clear," Ria announced, "but it looks like both sides are adjusting to our maneuvers and are sighting on us again. Several of the smaller craft are swinging around to flank us. Can't get a good read on them, but they look like a cross between a large fighter and a small bomber. They're quite agile."

"Any clue who these people are?" Reynolds asked.

"From the transmissions we're receiving between the combatants, the red and black ships—the fighter-bombers —appear to be invaders," Maddox said. "The destroyer fleet is the Krokus 4 Navy."

"Looks like the fleet is holding its own, but it's taking some good hits," Asya reported. "The red boys are packing some serious firepower on those little ships."

"Decision time," Reynolds stated, scanning the viewscreens and monitors for each and every detail.

The *Reynolds* had followed the trail of the Kurtherian energy signals they'd stumbled upon back at Grindlevik 3 to Krokus 4. It logically followed that they would help the Krokus 4 defenders because he needed to go planetside. The information wouldn't jump into his lap. He needed to go get it, and he couldn't do that if the planet got itself destroyed.

Reynolds' uncertainty came from the strange signals he was picking up from the invading force, as well as those from the planet.

"See if you can clean up that energy trace, Asya," Reynolds ordered. "I'm getting clusters of Kurtherian noise from both the planet and the attackers."

Asya's fingers flew over her console, and she shook her head a moment later. "No confusion," she confirmed. "There are hints of Kurtherian tech resonating from all the ships out there, as well as Krokus 4."

"Jackpot!" Tactical called. "Time to blow shit up."

More weapons fire strafed the SD *Reynolds'* shields.

"Some of the red boys are on us," Jiya reported.

"Take them out, Tactical," Reynolds commanded. "But *only* them," he clarified.

"You take all the fun out the job, Reynolds," Tactical complained, but he didn't hesitate to follow the order.

As the SD *Reynolds* swung about, Tactical triggered the railguns and loosed a barrage of fire on the attacking fighter-bombers.

Caught off guard, the first ship was blasted into space

dust. A nose-on blast from the *Reynolds* was more than its meager defenses could handle.

The second of the attackers veered at the last second to avoid the fate of the first. It managed to extend its life by less than one additional second.

The entire rear half of the ship was devastated and the ship bisected, sending the forward half tumbling through the blackness of space while the back flared out. The pilot's screams for help rang across the comm as the fighter-bomber spun away. The call went quiet when the remnants of the ship hit the atmosphere of Krokus 4.

"Suck on that," Tactical shouted. "Badass tactical officer: 2, toasted morons: 0."

"Don't throw a gear out trying to pat yourself on the back, Tactical," Jiya warned him. "We've got three more incoming."

The SD *Reynolds* shuddered in reply to an attack, confirming Jiya's words.

"You act like these guys are a threat," Tactical shot back. "Gravitic shields are holding steady. The enemy is lining up to get shot."

"Let's not underestimate these people, Tactical. Just take them out," Reynolds ordered.

"Gladly," Tactical replied.

The railguns fired again, sending projectiles through space at near the speed of light. They tore into the approaching fighter-bombers and two exploded; flashes of light flared, then immediately disappeared. The third ship had a huge hole blasted in its hull, the blast ripping half of the ship's port side away.

It listed and spun, crashing into the *Reynolds'* gravitic

shields. The superdreadnought shuddered under the impact but the fighter-bomber was obliterated, dust and debris skittering across the shields as if it were a celebratory light show. The superdreadnought continued through the destroyed ship's detritus to improve its tactical position.

"That had to hurt." Tactical laughed.

"The destroyers are counterattacking the rest of the red guys," Asya announced. "They're taking them out."

The crew watched destroyers annihilate the last three fighter-bombers.

"The Krokus 4 Navy is hailing us from their lead ship," Comm called.

"Now *that's* how you make an entrance," Tactical crowed from his post.

"On screen," Reynolds ordered.

The viewscreen lit up, and the image of a male alien appeared. There was no smile or indication that he was pleased to see the SD *Reynolds* or its crew.

"I am Colonel Gar Raf of the Krokus 4 Naval Fleet, commander of the *Alfar*," he announced.

Reynolds took the time to examine the being during the introduction.

Humanoid, the colonel's skin was so dark that hints of purple flashed under the lights that illuminated him on his bridge. His wide, round eyes were like pits of fire, burning crimson with dots of yellow at their center.

His outfit was crisp and regal, and his dark hair was cropped short, telling Reynolds that the Krokus 4 military was a proud one. The few crew Reynolds could see behind the colonel were similarly attired and postured.

"I am Reynolds, captain of the SD *Reynolds*, an Etheric Federation craft," he answered. "We come in peace."

"That's how every alien invasion film ever made starts," Tactical muttered, low enough that only the crew could hear him.

"We appreciate your efforts in ridding us of the Orau invaders, the pesky zignots you swatted…"

"Zignots?" Jiya asked XO over the comm, her translator not explaining the word.

"Hairy-ass dingles," XO told her, chuckling. "At least that's what the system is telling me it means."

Jiya made a sour face as the colonel went on.

"However, understand that we have our reservations about you, Reynolds," the colonel said. "You did appear out of nowhere in the middle of our fight without warning or explanation."

"Most certainly," Reynolds told him. "We were coming to your planet to negotiate terms on behalf of myself and the Federation for assistance with our mission," he explained. "Our arrival in the middle of the battle was a miscalculation on our part. My apologies for that."

Colonel Raf nodded. "Understood," he shot back. "However, I am not authorized to treat with you, Reynolds," he explained. "Our president, Jaer Pon, has issued explicit orders that I detain you and your craft in space until he deems otherwise."

As the colonel said that, Reynolds noticed that the fleet of destroyers began to crowd around them. Alarms flashed on the various consoles, warning that the Krokus 4 Navy was targeting the superdreadnought.

"So much for a friendly welcome," Jiya muttered. "Maybe one day."

"I wouldn't count on it," Tactical argued.

"I must confer with command," Colonel Raf told Reynolds. "Until then, I ask that you maintain your position and do nothing to make my people believe you are a threat."

"You mean besides us being a superdreadnought?" Jiya asked quietly.

"Should you violate this directive, we will be forced to destroy you," the colonel went on.

"Good luck with that." Tactical laughed.

Reynolds nodded to the colonel, accepting the terms.

"I will contact you once I have orders." Colonel Raf nodded, and the viewscreen flickered and returned to its view of the planet below.

"He doesn't think he can hurt us, does he?" Tactical asked.

"They have enough firepower to scratch the paint, though," Asya clarified.

"They may not be packing the biggest arsenal," Reynolds said, "but the impact is to the overall mission. We need to find out about their relations with the Kurtherians. If we fight them, then we have to take the information. If they share it willingly, we can get what we need and get out. I don't think there are any Kurtherians here, but they were here. Question is, how long ago?"

Maddox cut in, "Takal reports that some of the previously damaged shielding is damaged once again. He's got a crew on it already."

"Did someone paint a bright red X on the hull?"

Reynolds asked. "Or maybe a big bullseye? When we left High Tortuga, I envisioned something different."

"It's nice that you said 'we.' I'm getting teary-eyed over here."

"I've had about enough of you, Tactical. It pains me to know that you were birthed from my loins. Or digits, as it may be. I can't believe what I hear coming from your suckhole."

"What have you heard?" Tactical mused in a quiet voice.

"More than a polite person can repeat in mixed company," Jiya interjected.

"So, you're saying you have no problem repeating it for the world to hear, then?" Tactical shot back.

"You're lucky you're not real," Jiya muttered.

"As real as any of the boyfriends you claim to have had back home," Tactical joked.

Jiya covered her heart. "Ouch."

"Stow it," Reynolds grumbled, not up for listening to the back and forth. "Get us some information on the Orau, Asya. I want to know who and what these people are." He motioned to Jiya. "And scan the planet for intel we can use. We may get lucky and find what we need without having to play nice with these guys."

Both females went to work as Reynolds examined the planet on the viewscreen.

It was large, several times the diameter of Earth, but it was almost completely covered by water. The surface gleamed a brilliant blue, and their scanners flashed and bleeped as Jiya manipulated ship's sensors to reveal the planet's secrets.

It was Captain Asya who came back with the first information, though.

"The Orau are a nomadic race of beings, originally from the planet Oraunta," Asya reported. "Not a lot of information in the system, but these people are known for raiding and pillaging pretty much every place they come across."

"Vikings," XO exclaimed.

"I don't know what Vikings are, but if you say so," Asya went on. "Regardless, they've a reputation for being cruel and destructive. They raid a planet and eliminate the native leadership, then strip the natural resources. When they move on, there's little left. They leave destruction in their wake."

"Nice folks," Maddox remarked, shaking his head. "Guess we shot up the right bastards."

"Unfortunately, there's no way to be sure," Jiya stated, cutting in. "Krokus 4 is a blank slate with no detail. There is no information in any of the databases we've downloaded. No one has had any interaction with them."

"So, what *do* we know?" Reynolds pressed.

"That the planet is oceanic, obviously," Jiya replied. "The surface is ninety-six percent water, with only about two percent of the available land appearing to be habitable."

"Our colonel didn't look like a fish," Tactical said. "He part of that two percent?"

"I don't think so," Jiya answered. "The population of Krokus 4 is fairly small and condensed, most of them apparently living under the water's surface," she said. "There's only a tiny group of people scattered across the surface lands. I would estimate less than two hundred overall."

"Certainly not the makings of an army or a space navy," Reynolds mused.

"I would guess Colonel Raf isn't native to the planet, given his physiology," Maddox suggested. "Their tech appears to be quite advanced, though, so I can't be sure that something catastrophic hasn't happened to Krokus 4's native population in their recent history, forcing the surviving people to adapt to the new normal of living underwater."

"Speculate: how advanced?" Reynolds asked.

While he hadn't seen anything overly impressive among the fleet of destroyers surrounding them—their weaponry and defensive systems were standard—the fact that the vast majority of the people on Krokus 4 could live and prosper underwater told him there had to be some sort of advanced systems he might be interested in.

That opened the door to trade. They just had to get the Krokans to let them come down for a chat.

"As noted before, there are traces of Kurtherian energy signals emanating from the planet, but most of them appear to be coming from the ocean," Jiya said.

"Meaning that the tech that they're using to survive underwater is influenced by Kurtherians? Is that now or from the past??"

"Can't be sure how pervasive it is without closer examination, though," the first officer replied. "

"Which is the plan, if we can get Colonel Planetblock to let us come down," Tactical bitched.

"His people will see reason," Reynolds announced, although he wasn't as confident as he wanted to be.

"Or we kick in the door?" Tactical asked.

"Let's play it by ear before we decide to go storming the planet, okay?" Reynolds shot back, shaking his head. "Not everything has to be about blowing shit up."

"Blasphemy!" Tactical shouted.

"What's that?" Ria asked, pointing at an image she'd brought up on the viewscreen.

A space tug appeared from the other side of the planet, towing behind it what appeared to be a tiny space station. A tenth of the size of a Krokus 4 destroyer, the tow craft pulled it into open space a short distance from the super-dreadnought.

"Want me to blow it up?" Tactical asked.

"Didn't we just go over that?" Reynolds replied.

"So, is that a yes?"

"That's a no, Tactical." Reynolds sighed.

The tow ship released its cargo after making sure it was settled in place, then peeled off, returning wherever it had come from.

"Our host is back," Comm announced.

Reynolds motioned to bring it up on the main screen and Colonel Raf reappeared before them.

"President Jaer Pon has decided against allowing you and your crew to come down to the planet at this time," the colonel told them. "He has, however, graciously decided to send an envoy to meet with you and negotiate."

Colonel Raf motioned in the general direction of the floating station the tow ship had dropped off.

"We have provided a meeting location where the talks will occur," he continued. "A shuttle with our representatives will arrive shortly. We would ask that you send your own representatives over, and, please ensure that they are not armed."

"So, we're supposed to send people over to what looks like a floating trash can, unarmed, and trust that nothing shady will go on?" Tactical asked.

Reynolds groaned when he realized his other personality hadn't bothered to mute his question.

"Forgive my—" Reynolds started, but Colonel Raf only laughed.

"I understand your hesitation," he replied. "We give you our word that your people will not be harmed, and that we will treat with them fairly."

Reynolds nodded. "Then we'll meet with you," he replied. "As soon as your reps have arrived, we'll shuttle over."

The colonel nodded, still smiling, and cut the connection.

"Way to go, Tactical," Jiya complained. "Now they'll be expecting assholes."

"They wouldn't be wrong," he replied. "I just won't be among them." A quiet chuckle slipped out of the speakers above his position.

"Can't we replace Tactical like we have Helm and Navigation?" Jiya asked Reynolds.

Reynolds ignored the question. He wasn't completely sure at this time that he *could* reintegrate all of his personalities seamlessly, at least not while he was still constrained by the android body Takal had made for him.

While a marvel of technology, it barely contained

Reynolds as he was now. To connect the missing parts of his mind might well be too much for the body to take, and that might cause even more problems.

No, for now, the asshole part of his personality would have to stay separate.

"Ready a shuttle for us, Jiya, and get Ka'nak up and ready to go, as well as Geroux," Reynolds ordered. "Maddox and L'Eliana should go with us, too."

Maddox saluted from his station.

"That's a lot of crew you're dumping into a potential trap," XO warned.

"Well, if they do anything stupid, feel free to light them, their fleet, and their planet up as you see fit."

"Those are the kind of orders I love." Tactical laughed.

"You've got command, Asya," Reynolds told her, once again reminded of how he'd doubted her on the last mission. He was still making it up to her, but he figured putting her back in command made it clear he trusted her.

Jiya and the crew left the bridge and made their way toward the hangar bay, but Reynolds lingered a moment longer.

"A word, Asya," Reynolds said softly, crooking a metal finger for her to follow him off the bridge. Once in the relative privacy of the corridor he faced her, his features set and mouth grim. "I need you to learn more quickly. It's standard operating procedure to raise the shields before going through the Gate. We survived this one, but we may not the next. I need you to learn. I need the crew to learn. I need all you meatbags to gain personal experience so you can train future generations. You don't think one super-dreadnought can patrol this entire galaxy, do you?"

"I'm sorry," Asya stammered. "There is no excuse. Why didn't you stop me?"

Reynolds straightened and threw his chin back. "I am the Superdreadnought *Reynolds*. If you haven't figured it out, I have a certain arrogance. I don't think these creatures can beat me in any fight, straight up or otherwise."

"But SOP is SOP."

"Follow it," he ordered. "I am an integral part of this ship. Although I'll leave and the others will think that I'm not here except for some errant alter egos," he pointed toward the bridge with a head toss and a scowl, "I will always be here, but I'm giving you all rope. Don't use it to hang yourselves. You need to learn. The crew needs to learn. I'm giving part of my soul for you to manage, so don't hurt my fucking ship!"

"Yes, sir!" Asya blurted. Reynolds nodded once.

"Keep an eye out for more of those Orau craft," he told Asya, "and let us know if the destroyers or any of the Krokus 4 fleet does anything suspicious."

Captain Asya assured him she would, and Reynolds left for the hangar bay.

He was taking a chance meeting these people in an undefended box floating in orbit above the planet.

But that was what had been offered, so Reynolds would make do.

They'd had worse starts to their planetary adventures.

CHAPTER TWO

The shuttle's thrusters moved it silently from the hangar bay into space.

Geroux sat alongside her friend Jiya, and Ka'nak sat beside them. As usual, the Melowi warrior mimed throwing punches in the air in front of him, his trademark combat visualization.

Reynolds wondered if he should have Doc Reynolds check the guy's caffeine levels before a mission from now on.

He knew Jiya lived on the stuff, and she'd dragged Asya into her web of coffee-drinking madness. Ka'nak was already high-strung, which was probably what made him a good pit fighter.

Geroux was the opposite. Quiet most of the time, she'd huddle with Jiya and chat up a storm. The other times, she was usually nose down in her computer, working on some project or another.

Right now, she was working on the latest task that Reynolds had assigned her.

Given the Krokans' distrust of Reynolds and his crew, Reynolds wanted a safety net to fall into should something happen.

He'd set Geroux to hacking the peripheral Krokus 4 systems to get a better idea what they were facing.

He didn't want her to break in fully, because that was too risky. The Krokans might discover the hack, which would ruin any chance of a negotiation.

No, he wanted her to get the lay of the land, so to speak; work out a way to kick the door in if that became necessary. Until then, he wanted her to be subtle. To pick at the threads and see what unraveled without actually yanking on any of them.

She looked up and caught him staring.

"While high tech, their systems are fairly primitive," she reported, thinking that was what he wanted. "I've got reliable hacks ready for most of their systems, but there's some weird code I'm having trouble with."

"Where's that coming from?" Reynolds asked.

"The planet's surface," she answered, then paused. "Well, not exactly the surface. It originates under the water, but it's not coming from their primary city. It seems to be located a short distance away, basically out of nowhere. I can't detect any source mechanics."

"Is it a transmission?" Reynolds asked.

She shook her head. "No, more of an energy signal. Like the others, it's got Kurtherian traces about it, but it's definitely not Kurtherian. I'll keep working at it, but it's way different than what we're picking up from the primary

Krokan systems."

"Let me know if it changes," Reynolds requested.

She nodded.

"Almost there," Jiya called.

Reynolds glanced out the shuttle's window and took in the strange meeting place the Krokans had provided.

"It's pretty much…a box," Maddox stated.

"Doesn't look like much else, does it?" Reynolds asked.

"It has rudimentary shields protecting it from the elements, but it won't hold up to the barest of weapons fire should someone turn a gun on it," Jiya reported.

"You thinking it's a trap?" Ka'nak asked.

"It's tactically precarious," Maddox offered.

Reynolds shook his head. "Not sure what they think they'd accomplish by setting us up," he replied. "They have to realize the SD *Reynolds* is out of their league and would wreak havoc on their world if it were turned loose."

"That's presuming these people are intelligent," Maddox countered.

"There is that," Reynolds admitted, but he didn't want to think that he was leading his crew into a trap. "Be ready, just in case."

The crew shuffled in their seats as they stared out the window. They didn't like the idea of walking into something stupid any more than he did. And be ready…with what? They were unarmed.

L'Eliana stared straight ahead while the rest examined their destination. She wasn't ready for an adventure.

"You okay?" Reynolds asked her.

She nodded and swallowed loudly. "My first… Well, my

first just about everything," she admitted, laughing nervously.

Reynolds smiled. "Don't worry, you won't be expected to do much this trip. Maddox taught you how to operate the shuttle's autosystems, right?"

"He did," she assured, mumbling the steps under her breath.

"Then you'll be fine," Reynolds told her. "You stay in the shuttle and wait for us to return."

L'Eliana nodded. "Yes, sir."

"Everything will be fine," Reynolds reiterated, as much for himself as her. With growing trepidation, they closed on the Krokan station.

There wasn't time for more conversation as the shuttle aligned itself with the external dock attached to the small station.

Jiya glided the ship in easily, connecting the shuttle to the berth with the barest of *thumps*.

"We're locked," she reported. "Activating and pressurizing the boarding tunnel now." A low hum resounded through the ship, followed by a hiss. A moment later, Jiya tilted her head up. "We're all set."

Reynolds stared out the window at the Krokan shuttle that had arrived a short while before he and his crew had. Nothing about the other ship made Reynolds think it was anything more than a basic shuttle, designed to ferry passengers into or out of space.

"Watch that shuttle," he said over the comm to Asya, regardless. He was hopeful, but that didn't mean he'd make it easy for the Krokans to pull something if that was their intention. "You so much as see it light up on the scanners, you blast it."

"Yes, sir," Asya shot back.

"All right, people," Reynolds announced. "Let's do this. Ka'nak, upfront."

The Melowi warrior grinned and took his place at the hatch. Reynolds knew he was spoiling for a fight—that was his nature—but he was smart enough not to get them tangled in something they couldn't win.

Reynolds lined up behind him as the hatch hissed and peeled open, the landing ramp extending outward and clanging against the station's deck a moment later.

Stay sharp, Jiya passed over their internal comm.

Not detecting any weapons aboard, Asya told them. *Keeping their word so far.*

"Let's hope they continue to do so," Reynolds answered, waving Ka'nak forward.

The warrior walked through the airlock and into the station, his head on a swivel. Reynolds did the same, the crew crowding behind him as he surveyed the scene.

The small station was no more glamorous on the inside than it was on the outside.

Half the size of the SD *Reynolds'* hangar bay, the makeshift meeting hall was one big open space once they passed through the pressurization chamber.

They stepped out through a second hatch and were surprised to note that they could see everything in the place clearly. The station was brightly illuminated by overhead lights, and there was nothing to block their line of sight.

A large table, with chairs scattered around it, sat in the

center of the room. Six Krokan representatives stood on the other side of the table, staring at the crew as they arrived. There were what appeared to be three males and three females.

Like Colonel Raf they wore immaculate uniforms, ranks and insignia displayed proudly, though Reynolds had no idea what meant what. He could only presume the female at the center of the grouping was in charge, given where she stood and the confidence of her posture.

Their dark skin gleamed under the lights, reflecting purple when the right angle aligned. Their eyes shone brightly with inherent intelligence.

The Krokans hadn't sent a team of underlings to meet with Reynolds and his crew. That made the AI more comfortable.

Looks like a court-martial getting ready to happen, Maddox said as they made their way toward the table.

They are quite...decorative, Reynolds admitted.

They're comfortable, though, not tense, Ka'nak reassured them. *If humanoids are consistent in their body language, they don't look ready to start a fight.*

Good to know, Geroux said with a sigh. *The only weapon I have is my computer, and I'd hate to have to break that over someone's head.*

We'll be fine, Reynolds said, hushing them as they drew closer to their counterparts.

"Greetings, Reynolds and crew," the female announced as they came to a halt by the table. "I am Flor Alar, and these are my assistants Gol Ree, Ata Vi, Du Tho, Mar Son, and Elv Tin." She pointed to each as she said their name, starting with the females and closing out with the males.

Reynold named the crew in turn, introducing them.

"It is our pleasure to make your acquaintance," Flor stated.

"As it is ours," Reynolds replied pleasantly. Once they had gotten closer to the Krokans and could see them more clearly, he realized that they weren't as impeccable as he'd first believed.

Flor especially. Her eyes shone brightly, as did those of her assistants, but there was a quaver in them that Reynolds hadn't noticed in those of Colonel Raf.

She looked tired and worn. There were creases in her brow and cheeks that were hard to examine without staring, but Reynolds' advanced vision helped parse the details without looking as if he were conducting a medical examination.

Flor Alar was slim, wiry almost, as were the other Krokans, almost like they didn't eat enough. Veins stood out on the backs of their hands, and Flor clenched her fists over and over without realizing she was doing it.

A nervous tic, Reynolds thought, once again projecting his knowledge of humanoid races onto the Krokans. From what he saw, they *were* consistent. It was a nervous tic in a body that was under a great deal of stress.

These people weren't as confident as they'd originally appeared.

"Colonel Raf informed us that you are interested in trading with the Krokan people," Flor began. "What would you like to discuss?"

The Krokan representative waved everyone to seats, and the crew obliged, plopping down. The aliens waited until the superdreadnought's crew had taken seats before following suit.

"Forgive me," Mar Son asked, jumping in. "But are you…an android?"

Reynolds grinned. "This body is, yes, but I am not," he replied. "I am an artificial intelligence, an AI, inhabiting this form so that I might be mobile, but I'm also a part of the ship we arrived on, the Superdreadnought *Reynolds*," he explained. "We are inexorably linked."

He'd added the last as a warning to the Krokans, should they think they could separate the crew from the ship. He made it clear that wouldn't happen.

Mar Son nodded at his answer, seeming to understand the implied threat.

"Forgive our curiosity," Flor said. "We have never met with an android before."

"Nothing to forgive," Reynolds assured her. "This is no more than a husk to house a small piece of my consciousness. Rest assured, you are not treating with a simple machine."

"Can we ask you about the attackers in the red and black ships? The Orau?" Jiya interrupted, trying to redirect the conversation and maybe catch the Krokans off balance so they would give away information without realizing it.

Flor sighed. "They are a scourge upon our people," she replied, disgust plain in her voice. "They have attacked our forces and raided our planet for years, but no fight is ever straight up. Their attacks are sneak attacks, their raids are against the defenseless."

"Sounds difficult," Jiya comforted.

"It can be, most certainly," Flor explained. "Hence our

distrust of strangers." She glanced at the crew, her gaze landing on Reynolds.

"Understandable," he told her, "but we are not the Orau."

"That much is clear, seeing as how you did not return fire upon us despite our targeting your ship when you first arrived."

"We hadn't expected to appear in the middle of a war." Reynolds laughed. "As such, we can't hold your reactionary fire against you," he explained. "You ceased hostilities as soon as we broke off. That assured me that we made the right decision by engaging the Orau as we did."

"For which we are grateful, most certainly," Flor went on, "but, again, you must forgive us. We have to be certain of your intentions before we allow you anywhere near our planet or people."

"Of course," Reynolds told her, raising his hands to show he meant them no harm.

"According to Colonel Raf, you are here to trade with us? What would you be looking for?"

"We're on a mission for the Etheric Federation," Jiya explained, jumping in.

It was always good when she did. It put a more natural face on the negotiations, which could be easily derailed by strange beings made to converse with an android AI.

"While the details are our own, I'm afraid, our visit here is a peaceful one," Jiya continued. "Our mission takes us far into unknown space, and we make an effort to set up safe havens along our path and trade for essential supplies we might need as well as technology that will make it easier to accomplish, or at least more comfortable for the crew."

"And what do you think we have that fits that latter description?" Flor questioned.

"To be blunt," Jiya said, "the vast majority of your people live underwater. "Given the salt content of Krokus 4's oceans, you must have a fantastic filtration system, at the very least."

Flor nodded. "We do have a system that allows us to convert the ocean water to freshwater without difficulty, yes," she replied, "but I am not certain our president would be willing to part with its details so easily."

"Of course not," Reynolds replied, smiling.

He hadn't expected the negotiations to be simple. They never were.

"Well, we are nothing if not obliging," Reynolds told her. "Given the circumstances of our arrival, and what you've stated, it appears that you need a stronger system of defense to ensure that Krokus 4 can stand up to the Orau."

"And you can provide such a system?" Flor asked.

"We can indeed." Reynolds nodded, glad that Gorad had provided them with the blueprints for his defense ring. "It just so happens that our last stop provided us with the schematics for a planetary defense system, which can be used to automate your defenses and stop any and all future Orau assaults upon your planet and people."

Although Flor tried to hide her excitement, Reynolds could read it in her suddenly stiff posture. He'd struck a nerve in the Krokan rep.

Which was good, because he wanted to get down to the planet and investigate the connection they had to the Kurtherians. He wondered if maybe they were getting closer to finding them, or if this were simply another waystation on the path the Kurtherians had taken through the Chain Galaxy.

"We would be willing to trade that defensive system for your filtration system, as well as the promise of a sanctuary for the SD *Reynolds* to dock safely at any point in the future when we pass through your space."

Mar Son leaned in and whispered something into Flor's ear that Reynolds couldn't hear. She nodded in response before returning her attention to the crew.

"We will pass your request on to the president and his people," Flor announced, getting to her feet. Her people did the same.

"If you can provide us with what you say, I suspect President Jaer Pon will be willing to meet with you in person."

Reynolds rose, as did the crew, and he nodded. "We would be grateful to continue our conversation."

"Then please, return to your ship," Flor told him. "We will travel to the surface and petition the president on your behalf. Colonel Raf or I will reach out to you as soon as we have the president's decision."

"Thank you," Reynolds told the representatives.

They filed out and returned to their shuttle and the crew went back to their Pod, everyone departing the makeshift station.

On the way back to the SD *Reynolds*, Jiya stared out the window at the Krokan shuttle as it headed into the planet's atmosphere.

"This seems like a lot of effort to go through just to meet the boss," she complained.

"It means they're being careful," Maddox answered. "If I

were them, I'd be analyzing every scrap of information they've learned about us and everything we said in order to come up with a plan to take us out, if it comes down to that."

"Do you think this is a delaying tactic?" Jiya asked.

"Just like we thought the trip to the station was a trap, they think our fortuitous arrival and assistance is the same," Maddox explained. "They're slowing negotiations down so that they can examine us, just like we're trying to figure them out and decide what we really want."

"Which is to kill Kurtherians, but that's not something they're going to learn by scanning us or asking stupid questions," Ka'nak gloated, grinning.

"True, but they are going to continue to probe us," Maddox told the Melowi. "Our unexpected arrival is suspicious, no matter how you look at it. Our offering them the means to protect themselves against their enemy is even more so. They'll continue to be cautious, so we can't let our guard down even if they do invite us dirtside."

"Are you suggesting they'll try to take the tech from us rather than trade?"

Maddox shrugged. "I'm no mind reader, but I would be slow to trust anything they tell us at this point," Maddox continued. "Did you notice how worn down the reps appeared?"

"I did," Reynolds replied. "They're under a great deal of pressure, it would seem."

"And whether that's from the attacks of the Orau or something to do with their own government is something we might need to determine before we get in too deep. It could be a huge factor in what happens planetside."

"I agree," Reynolds stated. "You keep working on your hacks and be ready, Geroux. Should they invite us down to the planet, it's possible we'll need to play dirty to retain our advantage if they are under the assumption that we are simply a new face of their old enemy."

"I'm on it," Geroux replied.

"So, we're off on another adventure, huh?" Jiya asked.

"Wasn't that why you joined up?" Reynolds countered.

"It was," Jiya admitted.

"Then let's do this," Reynolds told her.

CHAPTER THREE

Hours after the crew had returned to the SD *Reynolds* and prepped for a trip down to the planet, the *Alfar* hailed them.

Colonel Raf appeared onscreen.

"President Jaer Pon has approved your visit to our planet," the colonel reported, "but there are conditions."

Reynolds had known that was coming.

"No weapons, I presume," he asked.

"Precisely," Colonel Raf replied. "We will allow you to travel to the planet in your own shuttle for convenience and to provide you with a sense of security, but there will be fighters escorting you down."

"Understood," Reynolds told the colonel. "We have no interest in harming your people, Colonel. We'll abide by your directions."

"Your cooperation is appreciated." Colonel Raf offered a thankful nod. "Send down your shuttle when you are ready. Our escorts are in place and waiting."

The screen flickered, and the colonel cut the connection.

"Still thinking they're planning something, Maddox?" Jiya asked.

"You never know," the general answered. "It certainly doesn't hurt that we've packed some of Takal's toys to take with us." He tapped the chest of the armor he was wearing.

One of the inventor's projects, besides trying to design a new and better android body and brain for Reynolds, was the creation of personal cloaking devices. Takal had modified them recently and they had miniaturized nicely, allowing them to be included in a suit of powered armor or carried by a person without it being obvious.

Unfortunately, Takal had been so busy with the agroprinter system that he hadn't been able to include cloaking devices in all of the suits. Only about half the crew had them.

Splitting his time between duties, he had, however, managed to minimize the obviousness of their armor suits, all while increasing the protection they provided. While Takal hadn't yet gotten to the point where the suits weren't obviously armor, they were far more maneuverable and sleeker than those he'd started with.

Using the special metals they'd collected on Lariest to craft the suits, the armor was far more effective than anything they'd had before, yet it hardly looked the part.

Once he was able to get all of them cloaking devices, the armor would be nearly perfect.

"Too bad we can't pack a bunch of guns to take with us," Ka'nak complained.

"Guess you'll just have to kill all the bad guys with your bare hands," Tactical told him. "You can do that, right?"

Ka'nak snarled toward Tactical's station. "Of course I can. Doesn't mean I want to, though," he replied. "Do you know how hard it is to get blood out from under your nails?"

"Can't say that I do," Tactical replied.

"Well, it's a right pain in the ass," Ka'nak informed him.

"Ever think to wear gloves?" Tactical questioned.

"Is this really the conversation we're having?" Jiya asked.

"He started it," Ka'nak muttered, pointing at Tactical's station.

"And I'm ending it," Reynolds told them. "Shut the hell up so we can get on with this." He sighed. "Asya, stay in touch with us on the comm and keep us on the scanner, and be sure to let me know if that shithead Loranian craft decides to pop back in."

"Hopefully those mines we left for them at our Gate points took care of that problem," XO said.

"We're not that lucky," Jiya argued.

"Probably not," Reynolds agreed, "so stay on your toes. We don't want a repeat of what happened above Grindlevik 3."

"Those destroyers out there aren't automated, though," XO clarified.

"No, but that doesn't mean the Loranians can't gain control of them," Reynolds replied. "With all the Kurtherian tech floating around these parts, it's better to be smart than dead. Who knows what they can accomplish?"

Reynolds started off the bridge. "Now, let's go, people. Places to be, people to negotiate with."

The crew followed him, and Reynolds wondered if he should include Takal this time around.

He thought better of it as they made their way to the shuttle.

Reynolds needed Takal to continue his work on both the new agroprinter system—the food supply system that would provide the SD *Reynolds* with fresh food no matter where they were—and the design for Reynolds' new body.

He flip-flopped on the priority of the two multiple times a day, but the inventor had assured Reynolds that he could work on both at once if he had sufficient help.

Reynolds had offered him San Roche, one of the Telluride they'd picked up on Grindlevik 3. Along with the prospect of having an army of bots and the maintenance crew at his beck and call, Takal was enthusiastic about the possibilities.

After everyone was aboard the shuttle, the crew set off for Krokus 4. Four Krokan fighters joined them as soon as they flew beyond the *Reynolds'* shields.

"They're not playing around, are they?" Geroux asked, peering out the window at one of the fighters.

"Nope," Jiya answered. "Two of them have us targeted already."

"Then let's just follow their directives and avoid giving them a reason to blow a hole in our collective ass," Reynolds suggested.

"Speaking of which," Jiya announced, "they're hailing us now."

She didn't wait for the order to open the channel.

Flor Alar's melodic voice sounded over the speakers. "Greetings again, Reynolds and crew."

Jiya returned the greeting.

"Coordinates have been transmitted to you," Flor told her. "Do not deviate from the flight plan you've been provided or your escort will be forced to fire upon you."

Jiya turned in her seat and raised an eyebrow at Reynolds. He shrugged and nodded, ordering her to do as she was advised. She turned back to the controls with a grunt.

Jiya acknowledged.

"We'll speak soon," the Krokan rep said before cutting the connection.

"You realize the coordinates they gave us lands us on some tiny-ass island in the middle of nowhere, right?"

"Well, I do now," Reynolds replied. "I'm sure they have a reason for us putting down there."

"Maybe they want us to swim in," Ka'nak suggested with a straight face.

Reynolds wasn't sure if he was joking.

"Let's hope not," he replied. "I might rust."

"Nice to know your priorities are in order, Reynolds," Jiya complained. "Don't worry about us drowning or anything."

"You know how to hold your breath, right?" Reynolds fired back.

"Maybe I should just crash us into the ocean now and skip the wait," Jiya growled.

"Please don't," Geroux said in a plaintive voice. "I can't swim."

Reynolds rolled his eyes. "You tell us this now?"

Geroux shrugged and stared out the window at the water-covered planet. "No one asked."

"Let's hope our hosts have something better planned than dunking us in the ocean," Maddox said.

Fortunately, they did.

Jiya followed the course down exactly, and the shuttle landed on a piece of land that wasn't much more than a sandy beach about the size of the SD *Reynolds'* bridge.

The landing gear sank into the sand until they hit something solid. The engines quieted.

"What now?" Ka'nak asked.

As if Flor had heard him, the comm warned of an incoming call. Jiya answered it.

"Thank you for complying," the Krokan rep said. "The next step will require the same level of compliance, or you risk both your ship and your crew."

Jiya bristled as if she'd been threatened, but Reynolds raised a hand for patience.

"What do you need from us?" Reynolds asked.

"You will need to shut your shuttle down except for your life support systems and minimal lighting," Flor advised. "These instructions must be followed for the remainder of your journey."

Reynolds signaled for Jiya to comply. He had no idea what the Krokans had planned for them, but he didn't hear a threat in Flor's voice, only a warning.

Once Jiya had complied, Flor spoke again.

"A protective shield will now cover your shuttle so that it can withstand the pressure of the water."

"Wait! We're going down there?" Geroux asked, pointing at the ocean.

"You will be safe," Flor assured, hearing her concern. "Barring your engines flaring or weapons fire, the shield is near impenetrable."

"*Near?*" Geroux said, eyes wide.

We're safe, Reynolds told her over the internal comm. *Even if their shield fails, which it won't, the shuttle is designed to survive and function underwater.*

Geroux looked slightly mollified, but not much. She swallowed hard and stared down at her computer, doing her best to ignore what they were about to do.

A loud hiss outside made that difficult.

The island expelled a clear plastic-looking substance that rose around the shuttle to envelop it.

Alarms sounded in the shuttle and Jiya silenced them, but the frustrated look on her face made it clear she wanted to fly them out of there immediately.

She didn't, though.

After several moments, the bubble appeared to solidify, and the alarm lights faded. Jiya checked the sensors.

"Life support is working fine in here, and the scanners aren't identifying any sort of threat emanating from the bubble that's sealed us in. In fact, there seems to be atmosphere inside the bubble. It's stable, from what I can tell."

That was when the ground gave way beneath the shuttle and it plunged into the ocean.

"You were saying?" Geroux gasped, clinging desperately to her seat.

Seconds later, the ship slowed, and the swirl of golden sand that had dropped away around them cleared from the water.

Encased in a see-through bubble, the shuttle hovered in place, nothing but crystalline water surrounding them.

"Sorry for the unexpected drop," Flor said over the comm, opening the channel once more. "The shielded craft you are currently docked on will take over the journey from here."

"A little late for the warning," Geroux muttered.

"Sit back and enjoy the rest of your trip," Flor told them. "I will meet you in the docking bay once you've arrived."

"Arrived where?" Reynolds asked.

"The capital city of Ocelora, of course," she answered.

"Of course," Jiya responded, exasperated.

"See you soon," Flor said, cutting the connection.

"No one's claustrophobic, are they?" Reynolds asked.

"Probably should have asked that before we left," Jiya shot back, shaking her head.

"Not like it comes up in normal conversation," Reynolds argued.

"Neither do chats about underwater cities and floating bubbles, but here we are," Jiya retorted.

"Wow!" Maddox blurted, interrupting them.

The general stared out the window, wide eyes reflecting the blue of the ocean.

The crew joined him, all except Geroux. Reynolds was as impressed by what he saw as Maddox was.

While Reynolds had expected fish and other lifeforms to inhabit the water, and there were certainly plenty of those in evidence, they weren't what Maddox was so enthralled by.

Bubble craft, which looked as if shuttles had bred with

glass, surrounded them as they made their way toward Ocelora.

Reynolds could see the pilots inside them, the front of the craft like the giant eyes of an insect. The pilots' dark skin stood in sharp contrast to the glassy composite of the ship, which looked as if it were a bubble being squeezed by a giant hand.

The metal frame of the ship had turbines it used as engines, leaving a swirling wash in their wake, and it also carried a number of weapons. The most obvious was a large harpoon gun mounted on the bottom.

"I hope that's for fishing," Jiya said.

"It's more likely for popping the bubbles of asshole visitors," Maddox suggested.

"I feel better already," Geroux whined.

"That shade of green looks good on you," Ka'nak told the young tech.

"It's going to look good all over *you* if you don't hush," Geroux warned while trying to disappear into her computer.

Ka'nak surrendered and let her be.

"That must be Ocelora over there," Maddox announced, pointing.

"It's beautiful," Jiya said, awestruck by the unique and alien architecture.

Reynolds studied it intensely, amazed at the sprawling underwater metropolis taking shape in the distance. He hadn't known what to expect, having never before seen a city under the waves, but he was certainly impressed.

A great bubble similar to the one that enclosed the shuttle encircled Ocelora, rising from the floor of the ocean as if it were a pair of hands cradling the city. All sorts of marine life swam around the protective bubble, but they stayed clear, never getting too close.

Reynolds wondered if there was something out there warning them off or if it was simple instinct, the animals realizing death lay beyond the barrier.

Either way, it was a sight to see as schools of brilliantly-colored fish skirted the underwater dome and veered off like sparkling flocks of sparrows.

"That's impressive," Maddox said, continuing to stare at the city as they drew closer.

Buildings towered inside the barrier, easily as tall as any Reynolds had seen in cities built on solid earth. He could see tiny craft flitting about, much like the fish in the water outside, skirting the edge of the dome while staying just within its boundaries.

Lights flickered beneath the dome, reflecting off the buildings and the darting craft. Distorted by the water and the hazy, ethereal nature of the barrier, it looked as if the makeshift sky were filled with tiny floating suns.

"If we could miniaturize this technology," Geroux said, overcoming her fear of the water long enough to sneak a glance at Ocelora, "we could use it for a host of applications, most of them not having to do with water."

Reynolds grinned at her, glad her love of technology had overcome, if only temporarily, her terror of the sea. He wondered what she and her uncle could come up with if they were to get the technology for the barrier.

As they drew closer, the automated bubble craft guiding them smoothly along, Reynolds began to notice cracks in the façade of Ocelora.

"Is that…" Jiya started to ask, then went quiet.

"Scorch marks," Maddox confirmed, inching closer to the window for a better look. "There are more over there," he pointed out, "as well as some damage near the top of the buildings."

"The place looks…bombed out," Jiya stated.

"It does," Ka'nak confirmed. "Guess Flor was serious about the Orau threat."

"Looks that way," Reynolds replied. More and more damage jumped out at them in stark contrast to their first impression.

Much of it looked recent. Some of it had been patched or repaired, but there was so much damage that it made Reynolds think there was an ongoing siege and not a one-time event.

That explains the haggard looks on the faces of the representatives, he thought.

"What could have caused all this?" Jiya asked.

"If I had to guess, I'd say a bombardment," Maddox answered. "Given the damage high up and the similar angle most of it appears to originate from, the city has seen several missile strikes over the past few months."

As the shuttle drifted toward a circular docking port jutting from the side of the dome, Reynolds saw even more damage. Much of it looked older now that they'd drawn closer and could better pick out details.

"Looks like it's happened a lot," Geroux muttered.

"I don't know if constant is the right word," Maddox started, "but it certainly happens regularly, given the nature and amount of the damage done. There's no way this is all recent." He gestured toward one of the taller buildings they could see. "That one there has been hit multiple times, based on the different materials used in the repairs."

"Lots of patches, no real repairs," Reynolds clarified, examining the surrounding buildings and seeing much of the same thing.

"I'm starting to get a good idea as to why they let us down here," Jiya offered, whistling. "Given all this, I can see an automated defense system sounding like a miracle right about now."

The shuttle slipped into the docking port with a gentle *thump*, quieting the conversation.

The crew stared out the windows to watch the process of docking.

The bubble craft eased through a short tunnel that connected the external dock to the city inside. As they reached the far end, the water in the docking tunnel drained away, pushed into the ocean behind them.

Once it was all gone, momentum carried the bubble craft through a thin, hazy barrier and into the city with an audible *pop*.

A platform rose from the ground and cradled the shuttle. It lowered the ship slowly. As it did, the bubble around the shuttle retracted into its base, disappearing completely by the time the shuttle settled on the landing pad. Then the platform wheeled the shuttle out of the way of the docking port and parked it near the edge of the tarmac.

A vehicle pulled up and several of the dark-skinned aliens, their uniforms resplendent, emerged. Smiles creased their faces.

Reynolds thought the expressions looked forced, but at least they were trying.

"Okay, people," he said, "let's go meet our hosts. Play nice," he added.

Jiya chuckled and triggered the shuttle's hatch and ramp. Once it was open and extended, Ka'nak went out. Reynolds followed with the rest of the crew behind him, Maddox bringing up the rear.

They left L'Eliana in the craft to watch over it and offer assistance as needed. She shut the hatch behind them, sealing herself inside. The host representatives came over as it closed, Flor leading the way.

A half-dozen guards walked rigidly beside her. While they kept their weapons holstered, pistols hanging at their sides, it was clear they were ready to use them if necessary. Their hands hovered lightly near their weapons.

"Greetings again," Flor said. Of all the manufactured smiles, hers looked the most honest, although Reynolds could still see the worry that creased the corners of her eyes.

"We're honored," Reynolds told her, and she nodded in reply. Reynolds thought he saw a flicker of appreciation in her eyes before she glanced away.

She motioned for the crew to enter the vehicle. "Please, step inside and be seated. I am to take you to President Jaer Pon directly."

The crew did as instructed and clambered inside. Reynolds went in last, settling on a seat beside Jiya. The soldiers climbed in afterward, with Flor entering the vehicle last and taking a seat across from Reynolds.

Now even closer than they had been before, Reynolds

was able to more clearly see the weariness in her. She defied it with perfect posture—chin up, chest out—but there was no mistaking the exhaustion that lurked behind her eyes.

Reynolds knew he'd made the correct choice when he'd offered Gorad's defense system to the Krokans.

They needed it.

CHAPTER FOUR

The ride to the presidential compound was uneventful, but Jiya and the crew got a much better look at the city than she suspected the hosts wanted.

Before they'd even left the tarmac, she'd spotted dozens of blast holes in the asphalt and charred ground all around them.

While she hadn't seen anything more than holos of the various wars that had been waged on her homeworld, she immediately recognized the damage done to the underwater city.

It was just as Maddox had said: bombardment.

The Orau had apparently done far more against the Krokans than simply invade from space. They'd tried to eradicate them by bombing the city and its people. The Orau were willing to kill civilians.

Attacking the innocent in their homes. The Orau were quickly gaining a new mortal enemy in Reynolds.

Away from the landing area, the damage was worse.

Jiya could see where repairs had been made, and many places where they were still in progress, workers on the streets doing their best to patch walls and fill holes.

The workers turned to stare as they passed, and Jiya noticed the same tiredness in their expressions. Whatever they had been through of late, it had worn on them.

"Is it…always like this?" Jiya asked, gesturing to the battle-worn city.

Flor sucked in a deep breath and let it out slowly, nodding all the while. "The Orau invaders have assaulted us for many years, but they've recently become more aggressive, more hostile, and more free in selecting their targets," she explained. "While we used to be forced to fend them off only a few times a month, it has become a near-constant thing of late." She sighed. "About every other day now."

"That's horrible," Geroux exclaimed.

Flor nodded her agreement. "It is for this reason President Pon wishes to speak to you," she explained. "He is not one to meet with visitors, but he believes your appearance might be fortuitous."

"Among other things," Reynolds suggested.

Flor shrugged. "He is not one to take chances, Reynolds," she told him. "He will see you and hope that you are telling the truth and offering our people a true means of defense against the Orau. If not…" She let her sentence drag out into silence.

Ka'nak slapped his hands together, startling everyone in the vehicle. "Boom?"

Flor grinned but didn't dignify the Melowi warrior's comment with a reply.

It was clear, however, that the unfinished sentence was a threat, and Jiya knew to take it seriously. These people were in the middle of a war they were losing. Their humor had fled with the arrival of the Orau.

Living as they did under the ocean, there was no escape.

As they traveled, Jiya's thoughts bouncing from theory to theory as she plotted escape routes, the Krokan vehicle slowed and entered the presidential compound through a tightly-controlled corridor.

It reminded her of her father's palace, and she felt a knot forming in her stomach at the thought.

She hadn't meant to think of *him*, but she kept noticing similarities in the worlds she visited. They weren't good similarities either, and that left her on edge.

She snarled under her breath and pushed her memories of her father aside. Jiya had left home to escape him, and she wasn't going to let him torment her in her own mind. He didn't deserve to live there rent-free. She made a mental note to visit Doctor Reynolds and discuss the topic.

The guards at the palace entrance waved the vehicle through, a great door opening before them and letting the crew and hosts inside. The doors slammed shut at their backs once they'd passed through.

Inside the compound, there was a distinct military presence, something that had been minimal in the town outside.

If the Orau managed to breach the dome and invade the city directly, the last line of defense would be the presidential compound. As large as Ocelora was, there was little hope of securing all of it quickly and easily.

The presidential compound, however, didn't have that issue.

Guards manned the walls behind them, and a great number of cannons were mounted within armored boxes that surrounded the compounded. Soldiers in a heightened state of alert watched the vehicle as it slithered past.

They, like all the other Krokans Jiya had seen, looked tired, but that didn't diminish their edge or their military professionalism.

These people were prepared to go to war at a moment's notice, and judging by the damage within the compound, it appeared they'd had to do just that more often than not.

The vehicle came to a stop outside what appeared to be a large foyer, an entryway into the main building of the compound.

The doors of the vehicle opened, and the soldiers and Flor climbed out in an organized fashion. The crew followed once Flor had her people in place and waved for them to join her.

While Jiya hadn't noticed the chill in the air when they'd exited the shuttle earlier, there was no missing it now.

Her breath misted at every exhalation, as did everyone else's—except for Reynolds, of course.

She was glad of the protective insulation in her armored suit. While it did little to keep her nose and cheeks warm with the helmet retracted, it at least kept the rest of her comfortable.

She could deal with a little chill on her face. It reminded her of camping.

Flor led the crew into the foyer through a pair of wide

doors that opened as they approached. As Jiya had expected, there was a squad of soldiers just inside.

Their hosts weren't taking any chances.

Jiya looked them over as Flor ushered them in. The Krokan soldiers didn't so much as blink as the crew walked by, their steely gazes following each movement of Reynolds' crew.

Once past the wall of armed soldiers, Jiya relaxed and took in the sights.

Jiya had been surprised when she had initially seen the town outside, before she'd gotten close enough to see its true condition. She was equally amazed by the beauty of the compound.

Art of all kinds adorned the walls, bright and cheery against the dull white paint of the walls and tiled floors.

Geroux gaped at it.

Statues of what appeared to be great warriors were situated in nearly every corner, dark-skinned heroes brandishing their weapons and standing defiantly. They had a slightly roguish appearance, as if those immortalized there had been more than great people; they'd been great characters, too.

The craftsmanship was superb, and Jiya could see the boldness of the subjects, the ferocity in their expressions.

What she didn't see was the tiredness of the Krokans surrounding her.

The artists had either chosen to smooth those blemishes away, or it hadn't been there when the statues had been commissioned.

Jiya felt the latter was more likely.

"These are the great leaders of our past," Flor explained,

gesturing to the statues. "We have a storied line of successors to the throne."

"The throne?" Jiya asked, catching the monarchial reference. It contradicted the current Krokan leadership role of president.

Flor offered an embarrassed smile. "Forgive me for not being clear," she said. "Our people were once ruled by a monarchy, but no longer. Not being used to strangers among us, I rarely find myself corrected since the people know of whom I speak. My apologies."

Jiya smiled back at her. She was beginning to like Flor despite the slight mousiness of her approach.

"President Jaer Pon is just this way," Flor said, waving them through yet another pair of doors that opened at their approach.

Again, guards stood at attention on the other side, ready to defend their president. Jiya wondered how well trained and effective they were, and she knew Maddox and Ka'nak were thinking the exact same thing.

It wasn't that she wanted to fight them to find out, she was simply curious.

They'd entered the lair of the unknown unarmed, and while nothing so far had made her feel threatened, she couldn't help but think about an unseen risk to her life.

Reynolds had gotten it through her head that she always needed to be ready, prepared to do what was necessary. Life and death were separated by a thin line of action and reaction. To drop one's guard meant to surrender to fate.

Jiya wasn't ready for that.

She'd fought too hard and too long to be where she was and *who* she was. She wouldn't give that up so easily.

Once they were inside the throne room—the similarities too great for Jiya to think differently now—the doors closed behind them. Flor led them up the carpeted center aisle past what appeared to be pews on either side, all of them empty.

A three-step dais occupied the far end of the room, and a large throne sat at the center of it. There was a smaller chair to the right of the throne and an even smaller one to the left.

Jiya noticed there was a mini-dais that lifted the central chair higher than the others.

Seated in the main chair was a male she presumed was President Jaer Pon. An older male sat stiffly in the smallest of the seats, and what appeared to be a middle-aged female sat in the one to the president's right.

She looked regal in a way the president didn't.

Her hair was long and straight, so dark as to swallow the light shining on it. Her eyes gleamed above the sharp shelves of her cheekbones, but they seemed somewhat dimmed, like Flor's.

Whatever the weight that burdened them, it appeared to press down upon everyone, regal and common alike. It apparently showed no favorites.

The older male looked worn too, but more due to his advanced age than any obvious stress. His hair was short and he was balding, although it was hard to be certain given the similarities between hair and skin coloring.

His one eye—the other was covered by a patch—barely held any fire at all. He stared at the approaching crew with stark intensity, but there was none of the brilliance she had seen in the rest of his people.

Perhaps he's going blind, she thought.

"Welcome to Krokus 4," President Jaer Pon announced as they drew closer. He rose to his feet gracefully.

Dressed in a military uniform much like those of his soldiers, the president was tall and lanky but powerfully-built, but he too looked a bit drawn. His cheeks were sunken, forcing his eyes to bulge slightly, and his jaw jutted like a granite cliff overlooking the sea.

"Mister President," Flor began, offering a shallow bow to person on the main chair. "I bring you the crew and captain of the Superdreadnought *Reynolds* of the Etheric Federation." She turned and pointed to each of the crew in turn. "This is Reynolds, the AI I told you about. Beside him is Jiya Lemaire, Geroux Durba, Ka'nak, and Adrial Maddox."

She stepped to the side, ushering the crew to the dais steps.

"May I present Minister To Gul," she said, gesturing to the old male, "Vice President Shal Ura and, of course, President Jaer Pon."

"It's our pleasure to meet you, Mr. President," Reynolds told Jaer Pon. The rest of the crew bowed their heads in greeting.

The president came down the stairs without hesitation, and Jiya saw his guards snap-to and move closer. He didn't seem to notice their disconcerted looks as he extended a hand to Reynolds first, then the others.

Jiya grinned as she shook his hand quickly, letting him move on to the rest of the crew. Once he was done, he didn't bother to step back. Jiya could see his guards weren't happy about that either.

While she didn't know enough about the president to trust him, she couldn't help but like his forthrightness. While he, too, looked as if it had been a long, long time since he'd enjoyed a good night's sleep, his smile appeared genuine.

It was the first real smile she'd seen since they'd arrived.

She certainly hadn't expected that to come from him.

Vice President Shal Ura came down to stand beside him once the handshakes were over.

"My assistant Flor Alar tells me you have come to negotiate trade between our people. Is that correct?"

"It is," Reynolds replied. "We believe there is much we can offer one another, especially given the circumstances into which we arrived."

The president nodded. "Yes, about that…"

Reynolds gazed at him expectantly, and Jiya made sure her expression was as neutral as it could be. Although they'd danced around their mission to Flor, it would be harder to do so with the president and not find themselves coming off as insincere.

"I have been tasked by my Queen, Bethany Anne of Earth, to track down and capture an escaped convict of some value," Reynolds lied. "We were tracking his energy signature and believed he had come this way," he explained. "We hadn't expected to arrive in the middle of a fight, nor had we any intention of involving ourselves.

"However, the attack upon our ship necessitated a response, and it was clear that the Orau were the aggressors. We responded accordingly."

"For which we are grateful," Jaer Pon told him. "Your timing was quite fortuitous."

"No more than a coincidence, I assure you," Reynolds went on, trying to diffuse any connection between the SD *Reynolds* and the Orau in the eyes of the Krokans. "We lost track of our quarry in the chaos and decided it would benefit us both were we to reach out to you and offer a trade."

Jaer Pon nodded. "Not the least of which, as Flor explained, is a defensive system that would protect our planet from Orau attacks?"

"Most certainly," Reynolds answered. "Since it is an automated system it would open none of your soldiers to risk while using it, leaving the fighting to a fleet of ships permanently stationed in orbit above Krokus 4."

"That sounds wonderful indeed," the president replied. "And in return for this system?"

"We ask for safe harbor in your space for future visits and food stores and basic necessities when we are docked here, and we would like to examine the technology behind your water filtration system."

Jaer Pon's eyes narrowed slightly. "I can guarantee the first two of your wishes, certainly, but I'm hesitant about the last, given the sensitive nature of the technology. Should it fall into the wrong hands, it might well be used against Ocelora and my people," he explained.

Reynolds said nothing, only offering a shallow nod as the president appeared to contemplate the offer before him.

Jiya wondered what he was thinking.

She hadn't imagined the filtration system knowledge

being used as a weapon, but that was her kindness showing.

She had no doubt that Maddox, Reynolds, and Ka'nak had already thought of a dozen ways in which the tech could be used against the Krokans.

Jiya glanced at Geroux and saw a similar thoughtful expression warping her features. She knew, however, that Geroux wasn't picturing destruction or death. Rather, she was picturing a multitude of ways she could put the filtration system to better use than simply installing one in the SD *Reynolds*.

Jiya smiled at her friend, the young scientist. Her kindness and generosity were but a few of the characteristics that made Jiya love her so.

The vice president leaned in and whispered something into the president's ear. He nodded in agreement or at least acknowledged he'd heard her, and turned his regal stare upon the crew.

"I find I must discuss this deal with my people before I commit to anything," he told them. "I cannot enter to such an agreement lightly."

"I understand," Reynolds replied, having expected that answer.

The Krokans needed to evaluate the quid pro quo.

"Flor Alar will show you to your quarters while I meet with my advisors and the vice president," Jaer Pon said. "Once we have made a decision, we will reach out to you for further discussion."

"Thank you," Reynolds told the president, backing away a step. The crew followed his example.

The president and vice president said their farewells

and returned to their seats as Flor ushered the crew out of the throne room and deeper into the compound.

After a short, winding walk, she led them past a handful of guards on duty before an opened door, waving them into the guest chambers beyond.

The rooms were simple, yet ornate in their own way. While they only contained the barest of usable furniture, there was art and statues and all sorts of tapestries and rugs bringing the rooms to a busy life.

While the rest of the compound had been tastefully decorated, these guest chambers were an example of excess. Flor remained standing by the door as the crew made their way into the suite of rooms.

"Servants will be by with food and drinks shortly," Flor told them. "Then, as soon as the president has made his decision, he will send me to collect you. Please make yourselves at home, and speak to any of the soldiers at the station down the hall should you need anything."

She turned on her heel and marched out the door, easing it shut behind her.

Jiya expected the sullen *click* of a lock, but there was none. Flor had left it unlocked, trusting the cadre of soldiers outside to keep the crew in place until she came to get them.

Jiya smiled at that.

She hated being locked up.

CHAPTER FIVE

"How could you not see the mine, Clevon?" Jora'nal asked, still furious that his helmsman had flown them directly into a trap laid by the Federation slags.

"Forgive me, master," Clevon begged, dropping to his knees before Jora'nal and clasping the hem of the captain's's robes. "Forgive me."

Jora'nal closed his eyes and drew in a deep breath to calm his fury. Clevon had served him well since they'd left Loranian space, but Jora'nal's master would not react kindly to incompetence.

It was one thing that the clever AI known as Reynolds had determined that Jora'nal's ship had been following their Etheric energy signature through the Gates, but it was another entirely to have the Federation ship set a trap for them.

Jora'nal let the breath out slowly. He reached down and set a hand on Clevon's head, resting it there. "I forgive you, Clevon," Jora'nal told him.

The helmsman sighed and slumped beneath his hand.

"Phraim-'Eh, however, does not forgive failure," Jora'nal stated, his voice cold.

He grasped a handful of Clevon's hair and lifted his head so that they were eye to eye.

"No, master. No!" Clevon shrieked, pawing at Jora'nal's hand, but it was no use.

Jora'nal drew a dagger from the folds of his robes and dragged it across the helmsman's bobbing throat.

Clevon screamed, the sound turning into the quiet burble of a river as blood and air spilled from the wound in his neck. He thrashed and kicked but Jora'nal held him fast, letting him slide around in the growing pool of his life's blood.

He stared at Jora'nal, still desperate to be forgiven. His eyes were wide with terror, yet there was still a kernel of hope there—a clinging, frenzied hope like a prayer on the lips of a person dying.

And that it was.

The hope died an instant before Clevon did, the life draining out of both and going dark.

Jora'nal released the former helsman's hair and let him fall to the deck of the Loranian cruiser. Final twitches racked the body, then it went still as Jora'nal stood over it, admiring his handiwork.

"Netri!" Jora'nal called without bothering to look away from the dead male at his feet. "You are our new helmsman. Thank Phraim-'Eh for his exalted generosity and take your position."

"S-sir," Netri muttered, his voice strangled. Jora'nal smiled as he heard the crewmember's whispered prayer to their god, amused to note that although the new helmsman truly believed in Phraim-'Eh, he had no expectation that the god could hear him.

Jora'nal laughed because he knew Phraim-'Eh heard everything through the Voice, his messenger, who'd come to visit Jora'nal and inspired him upon this pilgrimage.

"Someone clean this mess up and launch the body into space," Jora'nal ordered. "I will not be reminded of his failure, nor do I want to smell his stinking corpse any longer."

Several of the crew leapt to be the first to follow Jora'-nal's directive, desperate to avoid being the next sacrifice to the great god. Jora'nal grinned to see them clambering over one another in their desperate need to serve or their haste to avoid Jora'nal's anger. Fear kept them in line. Fear kept them on edge.

He knew they needed a lesson now and again—a reminder that Phraim-'Eh expected perfection of them—or their dedication to the god might wander.

Jora'nal couldn't have that. Their mission was too important.

But it was a fine line he had to draw between terror and discipline, inspiring his acolytes to action without pushing them into reaction or making them so afraid that they could not function.

"Excellent work," Jora'nal told the cleaning crew.

He offered them a toothy smile before turning to look at his XO, a haggard disciple by the name of H'ron.

"Report!"

"The mine was apparently cloaked, Master," he replied, voice strong and confident. "The *Reynolds* left it in the wake of their Gate passage, and we can presume there will be more should we choose to follow them directly."

"Then let's not do that, shall we?" Jora'nal replied, glancing at the new helmsman. "Set a course to follow the Federation ship, but stay wide of their exact coordinates to avoid another mishap."

"Unfortunately, Master," H'ron said, interrupting, "we will need to facilitate repairs before we Gate again."

Jora'nal spun on the XO, eyes blazing. "Why is that, commander?"

"The mine blew a sizable hole in the hull since the shields on that side of the ship were not activated at the time," he explained, although he intelligently kept his distance from Jora'nal. "Should we Gate with the hole only partially repaired, we will lose atmosphere and damage the ship even more, likely making us lose weeks, if not more."

"How long will repairs take, XO?" Jora'nal barked.

"The day, maybe less if I press the crew," H'ron answered.

"Then, by all means, XO H'ron, press the crew," Jora'nal told him. "Press the crew *hard*."

XO H'ron spat out an affirmative and stormed off the bridge to follow orders. Jora'nal returned to the captain's chair and dropped into it with a snarl.

He waited until his rage subsided and the furious quaver left his voice, before calling out to his navigator.

"V'ren, can you plot the course the Federation super-dreadnought took after they dropped their precious mine?"

"The exact course is easily tracked, Master—" the navigator replied.

"Which means there's another mine or two awaiting us," Jora'nal stated, cutting him off.

"Yes, exactly so, Master," V'ren went on. "Although I cannot accurately plot the follow-up course they took after Gating out a second time, I have an idea where they might have gone based on the nearby systems."

"Would you stake your life on this guess, V'ren?" Jora'nal asked, not even bothering to glance at him.

"I would," the navigator replied confidently, which pleased Jora'nal. "Of the three closest systems, only one emanates Kurtherian energy signatures, Master."

Jora'nal laughed. "Of course," he nearly shouted, realizing the navigator had to be correct. The SD *Reynolds* had been tracking the energy signatures, using them to point the way.

And perhaps that was how they spotted us, he thought, wondering.

"I presume we, too, project some measure of Kurtherian signal due to the makeup of our ship, correct?" Jora'nal asked.

"We do, although it is subtle," the navigator stated.

"Yet if the Federation ship can track Kurtherians across the galaxy, it must be enough for them to detect, wouldn't you think?"

V'ren agreed.

"Then perhaps we need to experiment with a way to shield our signature. Muffle it or perhaps block it entirely. What do you think, Navigator?" Jora'nal questioned.

"I'll investigate our options immediately, Master," V'ren told him, and began reaching out to various departments over the comm.

"Good," Jora'nal told his navigator, grinning all the while.

He activated the viewscreen and tuned it to show the ongoing repairs on the hull. Seeing the black char and wreckage soured his mood, yet he continued to watch for a few moments before finally turning it off in disgust.

A thought struck him.

"You stated that the Federation craft was tracking Etheric energy signals, Navigator V'ren, which was how you determined the likely location of the Federation ship," Jora'nal said. "Does that mean they went to the Krokus system?" he asked, picturing the star charts in his head.

"That would be correct, Master," V'ren replied. "I can't, of course, ascertain if they are still there, but that was their most likely destination. And should they follow their previous routines, they are probably still there interacting with the locals."

Jora'nal chuckled. "If it's interaction they're after, perhaps we should assist them," he suggested.

"How so?" V'ren asked.

"The most likely destination for the Federation slags would be Krokus 4 if I remember my charts correctly."

"That would be my guess, Master," V'ren replied.

"Then I think it is time to send a message to our allies in the area," Jora'nal told the navigator. "Bring up a subspace channel for me. I will reach out to see if our quarry has alighted in the Krokus system," he said. "If so, then I believe we might be able to earn back the day we're losing due to repairs."

Jora'nal let out a loud bark of a laugh.

"And perhaps we can pay them back for the indignities they've forced upon us while we're at it."

"Channel open, Master," V'ren announced.

Jora'nal waved him to silence, reaching out across space in hopes of a miracle.

Phraim-'Eh will provide, he assured himself.

And soon there would be blood.

CHAPTER SIX

Ka'nak went to say something, but Geroux hissed, stopping him short. Jiya elbowed him in the side for emphasis when he looked as if he might ignore her warning. He glared at her until she sent him a message across the private comm.

The room is bugged, so don't say anything, she told him, gesturing to Geroux.

Geroux casually held up the computer attached to her arm and showed him the flashing red lights on its display. There were a lot of them.

Ka'nak's eyes widened for an instant before he got them under control and nodded. Once more his mouth opened, but it closed right after, his message coming through.

I hate these things, he complained.

Jiya chuckled. She was the complete opposite, loving Takal's upgrades on the translator and comm devices. They were a single device now, and they allowed the crew to think at the device directly—which took some practice to get used to—and it then translated their thoughts into words and sent them over the chosen comm channel.

It wasn't telepathy in that the device didn't read others' thoughts, but it was effective enough that the crew could communicate with one another without ever having to say a word aloud.

With a well-trained team, the mental communicators could work miracles. With the current crew, they worked all right.

Jiya chuckled at the thought and smiled at Ka'nak while he scowled.

The crew examined their surroundings, Geroux and Reynolds circled the quarters, noting where all the bugs were located.

It took them a while.

Ten minutes after they'd started, they casually made their way back to the rest of the crew.

"I wonder what kind of food they'll provide," Geroux mused aloud, sending her real thoughts a second later. *This place has more bugs than a gralflie farm.*

Cameras, too, Reynolds added. "I'm sure the local cuisine will be quite to your liking."

Jiya and the crew carried on a double conversation the entire time, talking about inane and basic things out loud, things they had no real concern about the president over-hearing, while they spoke to one another over the comm link.

Seems like the nice guy act by the president isn't quite real, Geroux stated.

No, Jiya agreed. *This looks like next-level paranoia to me.*

I wonder what this means for said.

Could mean anything, sadly, Rey *we avoid saying anything that will anything other than what we say we a*

Well, we are *exactly what we've bullshit in the backstory,* Jiya told him

That might be true, but this is ⌐ⱼ *perception,* Reynolds fired back. *We are whatever* he *thinks we are.*

Which means we need to be on our best behavior, Jiya agreed.

The whole crew glanced at Ka'nak.

He felt them staring and looked up with a growl. *What?*

Maybe we should look for a safe zone in one of the rooms. Find a corner where the cameras lack coverage, Maddox suggested.

Good luck with that, Geroux remarked. *This place is wall-to-wall coverage.*

What do you have in mind, Maddox? Reynolds asked. "Perhaps we should try to get some rest until they come to collect us," Reynolds suggested aloud.

Jiya realized the AI wanted them to lie down so they could feign sleep and wouldn't have to keep up the double conversation, since their concentration was failing. The crew were getting quieter and quieter as they focused more on the internal monologue, which made them look even more suspicious than if they were talking aloud.

"I claim the couch!" Ka'nak shouted, stretching out and rolling over, burying his face in the cushions.

A quiet snore sounded a moment later.

The rest of the crew laughed and climbed to their feet,

separate rooms as if to look for a place to

job, Ka'nak, Geroux told him.

hen he didn't answer, she messaged him again.

Did you hear me? she asked.

Maddox chuckled in the other room. *He really* is *asleep, the lucky bastard.*

Reynolds remained in the main room, and Jiya could see him from where she sat on the edge of the bed in another room. Geroux came over and flopped on the bed behind her, face in the pillow.

I wish I could fall asleep that easily, Geroux remarked.

You and me both, Jiya replied, stretching. She didn't think she'd ever sleep again.

Anyway, back to my question, Maddox, Reynolds course-corrected the conversation. *What were you planning?*

I was just thinking it might behoove us to have someone cloak and slip out of the room to get a good look around, Maddox answered.

If there weren't so many damn cameras everywhere, I'd say that was a great idea, Reynolds told him. *Unfortunately, Geroux is correct. Our hosts' paranoia has ensured that there are absolutely no angles in the room that aren't covered by at least one camera.*

What if we short them out? Maddox suggested. *Maybe just one or two?*

With this kind of setup, whoever the president has covering the monitors would notice immediately, Geroux interjected. *You don't have a system this elaborate and leave it to automatons to operate it. This is a hands-on operation, guaranteed.*

Can you hack it? Blind the system without them realizing? Maddox asked.

Jiya felt Geroux shake her head on the bed behind her.

No, I don't think so, she answered. *I mean, I can kill the power and black the cameras out, seeing as how they seem to be connected to the primary power source in the compound, but there's no way to do it subtly.*

A knock at the door interrupted their conversation.

Reynolds got up and went to the door. Jiya came out of the bedroom a second later to back him up.

A smiling face greeted them when the door was opened.

"Good afternoon," a female said, nodding enthusiastically at them. "I am Kah Dur, headmistress in charge of visitor affairs."

Jiya peeked over Reynolds' shoulders and saw five more of the president's servants there, each standing behind a cart laden with food or drinks.

"May we come in?" Kah Dur asked.

"Certainly," Reynolds replied, stepping out of their way. Jiya did the same as the servants wheeled the carts into the room.

Think we can trust it? Jiya asked the AI.

We'll scan it for foreign substances, he answered, *but I don't think Jaer Pon would resort to poison when he has us dead to rights in the room, unarmed.*

I feel better already, Jiya said over the link, wishing Takal could add in a way to translate sarcasm across the system. The monotone voice lost a lot in translation.

Kah Dur directed the servants where to put the food,

and they worked to arrange it neatly and out in the open so the crew could see it plainly.

"Utensils and napkins are on the last of the carts," she pointed out, "and if there is anything else you might need, please ask one of the guards outside to send me, Kah Dur, a message. I will respond immediately."

She smiled widely, and it almost looked real to Jiya.

As soon as the servants were finished arranging the carts, Kah Dur chased them from the room, shooing them away like errant children. When they were gone, she turned to the crew and opened her mouth to say something, raising a hand...

The room went dark right then, the power flickering and going out.

Kah Dur eased the door shut behind her.

Jiya started forward on Reynolds' heels, each realizing the loss of power and Kah Dur's visit were not a coincidence.

"Wait, please," she called before they got to her. "I'm only here to warn you," she explained.

All the bugs and cameras are dead, Geroux reported from her room. *Power failure deeper in the compound, it looks like.*

"Everyone okay?" Maddox asked, stepping into the hall.

"President Jaer Pon is not who he says he is," Kah Dur told them, the smile gone from her face. "You are in danger here on Krokus 4."

"Why are you telling us this?" Jiya asked.

"Because I would not see you harmed simply because you stumbled upon the wrong location at the worst of times," she replied. "You must believe me: this world is not safe for strangers."

Geroux came into the room, still scanning for bug or camera activity. *We've got about twenty more seconds before the backups take over,* she warned. *The system is repairing whatever knocked it out.*

"Stay here in the compound and do not let the guards lead you anywhere else. It is too dangerous," Kah Dur warned. "There are far too many eyes on the room for him to harm you here, but elsewhere..." She let the rest of her warning hang unfinished.

Ten seconds, Geroux called over the link.

Kah Dur, as if able to hear Geroux's countdown, shook her head and eased the door open. "I must go," she called over her shoulder, racing out into the hallway as if her life depended on it.

Jiya wondered if it did.

Soldiers burst into the room an instant later, weapons drawn as the lights flickered and the power returned.

"I'm Sergeant Gib. Is everyone all right?" the soldier asked, eyes scanning the room.

"We're fine," Jiya answered, doing her best to look dumbstruck. "What happened? Are we under attack?"

Other soldiers circled the chambers, looking for anything out of place. They returned to the sergeant's side a moment later, shaking their heads.

"Looks like a simple power failure," the sergeant reported. "Happens now and again thanks to those bastard Orau," he complained. "Everything should be back to normal now. Nothing to worry about. We'll be outside should you need anything."

These are not the spies you're looking for, Reynolds

69

mumbled over the link as the soldiers left the room, shutting the door behind them.

What the hell are you on about? Jiya asked.

Nothing, Reynolds shot back, but that didn't stop him from grinning.

Maddox went over and flopped into a chair across from the still-sleeping Ka'nak. *You think she's credible?* he asked. "That was strange," he said aloud, regarding the power outage.

Geroux returned to the room, signaling that all the bugs and cameras were functional once more, and Jiya went to examine the food.

"I would imagine it happens fairly often, given Ocelora's location in the ocean," Reynolds said. "It must take a lot of power to keep the system up and functioning."

Reynolds shrugged as if it were meant as part of his public answer.

I don't know, Maddox, he answered over the link. *We've seen a hint of their uncertainty, given the number of devices in this room alone. We can't presume anything at this point, so it probably serves us to examine what Kah Dur said if the opportunity presents itself.*

Lots of activity on the security systems in here, Geroux reported. *They're checking on us after the power loss.*

Hopefully, they don't think we're responsible, Jiya added from the other room.

I don't think so since the source was nowhere near here, Geroux assured her friend. *I mean, yeah, I could have killed the power like that from here, but these people don't know that.*

I wonder if we can take advantage of it if it happens again?

Maddox said. *We could call Kah Dur back under some other pretense.*

I suspect Kah Dur feels she has done her duty and we won't see her again, Reynolds said. *She took a risk killing the power while she was here, and I doubt she'll try it again anytime soon. It would be too obvious that she was involved.*

It might already be obvious to security, Jiya exclaimed. *There wasn't a lot of subtlety in that.*

I agree, which is why we can't summon Kah Dur needlessly, Reynolds told the crew. "She risked her life to warn us, and it's not right for us to put her in further danger.

Then what do you suggest we do? Maddox asked. *With us stuck in these rooms, we don't have a lot of options.*

No, we don't, and we have to decide how to react to Kah Dur's warning, Reynolds answered. "She suggested we stay put for a reason. It's simply a matter of whether that decision is the smart one to make.

If we can't speak to her, there's not much for us to go on, Maddox stated. *Perhaps we could—*

A distant explosion went off, and the power in the room flickered once more. Second and third explosions were felt right after. Each sounded closer than the last, and the floor shuddered beneath their feet.

"What the fuck is that?" Jiya asked, racing out of the room with Geroux at her side.

The noise even woke Ka'nak. "Sounds like Ocelora is being bombed," he explained calmly, yawning as if it were an everyday situation for him.

Maddox jumped to his feet as yet another explosion erupted nearby.

"The city *is* under attack," Maddox called, realizing that

Ka'nak was correct. "Has to be the Orau again. They've come back for revenge."

Yet another explosion sounded, this one even closer.

"I don't know about you, Reynolds, but I'm thinking us staying here is a bad idea," Maddox suggested.

"I agree with you," Reynolds replied, motioning toward the door. "Let's get the fuck out of here before the dome is blown and a trillion metric tons of water drops by for a visit. Where is my ship?"

When they reached the corridor, they found it empty except for Sergeant Gib.

CHAPTER SEVEN

Sergeant Gib waved to the crew to follow as he ran from the palace.

The soldier rushed through Ocelora as missiles poured down upon it. The crew followed close behind, eyes on the watery "sky."

With every blow to the protective dome that held the ocean at bay, hundreds of gallons of water spilled into the city, raining down in great gushes before the barrier sealed itself.

"Definitely the Orau," Reynolds stated as they ran, dodging down random alleys to avoid being hit by direct fire or falling water.

"Are they always this aggressive?" Jiya asked the Krokan sergeant.

Gib shook his head, not bothering to glance back at Jiya. "No," he answered. "I can't recall the last time they lashed out like this."

"Guess we pissed them off," Ka'nak said.

"We have a knack for doing that," Jiya admitted.

"Where are you taking us, Sergeant?" Reynolds pressed, wondering if this was some part of the plot Kah Dur had spoken of.

They were out in the open now, just as she had said, and Reynolds began to think the soldiers might well be leading them somewhere better to dispose of the crew than the palace.

He hoped that wasn't the case that he was just paranoid, but either way, he would be ready.

No one would ambush his crew without his taking a pound of flesh from their hides.

"If even only a little of this is what happens during a normal bombardment," Geroux said as she sprinted along, "I can understand why everyone is so beaten down. This has to wear on you."

Reynolds agreed. "There's no living comfortably under such a threat," he stated. The Orau were relentless, and their constant efforts to tear down Krokus 4 were having an effect.

Even if the Orau failed to invade and pillage Krokus 4, they were winning the war by simple attrition.

From a distance, they could batter the Krokan people without much fear of reprisal, raining down terror over and over until their spirit broke.

It sickened Reynolds, and if he could do something about it before he and his crew left, he most assuredly would.

The Orau would pay for what they were doing to the people of Krokus 4.

"How much farther?" Maddox asked, desperate to catch

his breath.

He'd spent a long time in the dungeons of Jiya's father and had yet to fully recover from his ordeal despite the effort of the Pod-docs aboard the SD *Reynolds*. Without pumping him full of nanocytes, the general was only flesh and bone.

Reynolds had pondered upgrading the crew, but he'd thought better of it when he pictured Bethany Anne's expression when he informed her that he'd used nanocyte technology on people he'd known for only a short while.

She wouldn't take it well, he knew, so he had discarded the idea.

Maybe the day one of his crew got badly hurt when they didn't need to would expedite his decision. He had instilled in them that they had to bring everyone back to the ship. With the Pod-doc, he'd be able to heal them no matter what.

A missile struck a short distance ahead of the crew then, exploding and hurling shrapnel and flames their way. Reynolds wondered if now would be the time.

The crew sealed their armor by reflex, helmets closing over their heads, and darted for cover. Debris clattered around them, tearing at the walls of the building they'd hunkered behind.

Most of the soldiers weren't so lucky.

The sergeant squeezed in beside the crew, having been right on top of them, but the soldiers who'd been leading the way were caught in the blast. Fire lapped at them, tearing through their simple armor as if it weren't there.

Then a rush of water put them out, crushing them in the process.

Reynolds saw Geroux cover her eyes and duck away as the males died and crumpled to the ground.

He was grateful they'd expired quickly, none of them even getting the chance to scream as they were enveloped first by the fire, then smashed by water.

Black smoke roiled around as the chaos of the missile strikes settled. Reynolds was glad for the improved optics on the suits, which would allow his people to see no matter how bad it got out there.

But it wasn't the smoke they had to worry about.

Another missile exploded near the first, and a second and third followed. The path they'd been following was decimated in an instant, the nearby buildings exploding and toppling to the ground.

It was as if there had been an earthquake, the ground shaking and dancing beneath them, making it hard for the crew and the sergeant to stand. They leaned against the building at their backs and hoped it didn't get blown away like the others. Water pooled around their feet.

"What's going on?" Jiya asked, looking at Reynolds, who braved the carnage to stand nearest the corner where he could see out to the street.

"Our path is blocked," he replied, glancing at the sky. "And there are more missiles incoming."

"Shit," Maddox muttered. "And to think I just changed my underwear."

"Likely going to need to change it again if those damn Orau keep this up," Ka'nak informed him.

More missile strikes tore the city apart as the crew remained in place, unsure whether they wanted to run back the way they'd come or try to find a way ahead.

Sergeant Gib seemed a little more certain about what they needed to do.

"We need to get to the shelter," he stated matter-of-factly. "They're waiting for us."

"They who?" Reynolds questioned.

"The elites," he answered without hesitation. "The president and vice president and his council. It's the only place we'll be safe."

Reynolds watched the sergeant's expression for any hint of deception, but he didn't see anything that made him think the guard believed anything other than what he was saying.

That didn't mean the destination wasn't a trap or an ambush, but the soldier didn't know it was anything other than a place of safety.

"Which way?" Reynolds asked.

"We have to go out and around—" he started, leaning out to show Reynolds the direction. Gunfire rattled over his head and sent him scurrying back behind cover.

Reynolds took a shot to the chest and stayed in place a moment longer to see what was going on.

He growled when he did.

Ahead of them were a cluster of soldiers dressed in red and black armor.

The exact same color as the Orau ships that had attacked them in space.

"Orau," Sergeant Gib unnecessarily confirmed.

"Damn it!" Jiya spat, hearing the sergeant. "We don't have any weapons."

Maddox reached out and snatched the pistol from Sergeant Gib's holster.

"Now we do," the general claimed, leaning out from behind the wall and blasting the nearest of the Orau invaders.

The alien dropped, caught off-guard by the attack, but his armor was better than the armor of the Krokans. He scrambled to his feet again as Maddox jumped back behind cover, the Orau returning fire.

"That didn't go as planned," Maddox muttered.

"Pull back," Reynolds ordered, pushing them behind him.

Before they'd managed to flee even a step or two, an Orau soldier rounded the corner and raised his weapon.

It was the last thing he ever did.

Reynolds' fist crashed through his helmet's visor and slammed into his face.

There was a crunch of bone and the soldier went stiff, held aloft by Reynolds' hand in his gore-filled helmet.

The AI grabbed his pistol and handed it to Jiya, then flung the soldier's body at his companions. It crashed into the others.

"Get my people to safety, Gib," was all Reynolds said before he shot off.

He snatched a piece of broken brick off the ground and hurled it at the entangled Orau invaders. The brick crashed into the visor of one and knocked him back, gunfire blasting upwards as he fell.

Reynolds dropped to the ground and slid into the mass of soldiers trying to slip free of the dead person in their midst.

They didn't manage it.

Reynolds snatched a weapon from one of their hands

and turned it on its owner. Two quick bursts to the male's head left him with a charred skull and little else.

The other Orau scrambled to shoot Reynolds, but they were caught within the tangle of their companions, unwilling to blast their fellow soldiers to get free.

Reynolds had no such compunction.

He pressed the gun to the dead body and fired over and over, drilling holes through his armor and flesh and blasting the soldiers behind him.

The fight was over in a moment, the handful of Orau invaders lying dead on the ground.

Reynolds jumped to his feet, grabbed as many pistols as he could carry, and raced back to where the others were slowly making their way toward the shelter Sergeant Gib had promised.

The AI arrived just in time.

A group of Orau were in front of the crew and Sergeant Gib, pinning them in place. Maddox and Jiya were on opposite sides of the street behind different buildings, the two working in tandem to keep the Orau at bay.

One would fire and step back, then the other would, the pair alternating and mixing it up so as to not give the enemy the opportunity to predict which one would pop out next.

Reynolds came up behind the crew. "At your back!" he warned, passing the guns out as if they were party favors. He even gave one to Gib.

As soon as he'd finished, he darted across the street in a lull of fire, drawing the attention of the Orau.

He crashed into the wall on the other side, unharmed,

but what he'd seen when he'd been on the street gave him pause.

"We've got more incoming," he announced.

"How many?" Maddox asked.

"A bunch," he answered with a sneer.

"That's a pretty damn vague answer," Jiya complained.

He didn't argue.

The odds weren't in their favor.

While missiles rained down in the distance, battering the city, it appeared as if the Orau had figured out how best to land an invasion force without it being shot down en route.

Mixed among the missiles were tiny troop carriers.

Although they contained only three to four soldiers packed in tightly, the carriers came on the heels of the missiles, letting the ships flare out and land without resistance and eject their battle-ready contents into the streets in the wake of the explosions.

Reynolds had seen at least twenty of the ships inserting via the missile barrage nearby, and he didn't need to do the math to realize just how outnumbered he and his crew were.

"Can you reach your troops?" Reynolds asked Sergeant Gib.

The sergeant shook his head. "No comm," he answered, tapping the side of his head where a spattering of blood resided.

Reynolds growled. They were being hung out to dry, trapped in a city they didn't know, no allies anywhere.

"Can you fire on coordinates if I provide them?" he called up to the *Reynolds*.

He was sure he knew the answer before he'd asked, but he was still disappointed to hear it.

"Only if you and the crew want the entire ocean coming down on your head," Tactical replied. "Anything we do from here will rip open the protective dome and kill all of you in one big splash."

"Fuck a walnut," Reynolds cursed, leaning out to fire at the encroaching Orau to try to slow them again.

"What about L'Eliana?" Jiya asked over the comm.

"Given her inexperience and our lack of open space, she's more likely to shoot us than anyone else," Reynolds answered. "Besides, she wouldn't reach us in time, even if I let Helm take over the piloting."

Jiya leaned out and fired a barrage at the Orau. She dropped one, blowing a smoking hole in his chest after repeated blasts. She ducked back as they returned fire.

"Anyone got any grenades?" Ka'nak asked.

Ka'nak ducked and squeezed off a few useless rounds before he was driven back to cover.

"We're not going to get past these guys," he stated. "There are about twenty more moving up to reinforce them."

"We need to think of something fast," Geroux shouted. *Maybe we can cloak and flank these guys,* she said over the comm, so Sergeant Gib didn't hear her.

All we'd do is split our forces since Ka'nak and Jiya don't have devices, Reynolds replied. *We'd only kill ourselves quicker.*

Geroux growled her disappointment.

The young tech had been pecking away at the enemy, the barrel of her gun angled around the corner as she pulled the trigger with reckless abandon, but her efforts had done little to repel the enemy. She was getting desperate.

"Got any computer tricks up your sleeve?" Jiya asked.

"If you're asking me if I can hack the soldiers or their guns, the answer is a resounding, 'Fuck no!'"

Reynolds felt the pressure mounting. He'd unintentionally walked his crew into a killing field, and he had no idea how to get them out without putting them all at risk.

Well, more risk than they already had to worry about.

He contemplated his options, then decided the only viable choice he had was to delay the approaching Orau and give the crew a chance to retreat.

It was a slim chance, he had to admit, but it was better than standing their ground and ending up dead one by one.

I'm going to distract them, he announced over the comm. *As soon as I have their full attention, I want all of you to follow Sergeant Gib somewhere safe, if only long enough for Asya to send a crew down to get you and L'Eliana.*

What the hell are you going to do? Jiya asked. The look on her face made it clear she knew it was something stupid.

She wasn't wrong.

This is an order, he told her, not willing to get into it with her right then.

The longer he waited, the more likely it was that they would all be killed.

Just fucking do it, he demanded, then stepped out from behind cover and started forward at a run, blasting as he went.

The Orau took the bait and targeted him as he advanced.

Reynolds wasn't going to make it that easy.

He dodged and feinted and rolled and made himself as difficult a target as possible. As he did, he snatched up a second gun and fired both weapons into the crowd of Orau marauders.

He killed a number of them, but there were simply too many.

Their blows began to take a toll on his android body.

A shot to the chest made him stumble and a second one put him on his ass.

"Reynolds!" Jiya screamed, and he knew she was going to disobey him.

"Don't you fucking dare," he shouted back, climbing to his feet as another blast struck him center mass.

He growled and returned fire, smoke swirling all around, and that was when he realized the number of Orau who had just been standing in front of him had been cut in half.

"What the shit?" he exclaimed, having no idea what had happened. *He* certainly hadn't mowed through them like that.

As he sighted on an Orau soldier, he caught a flash of shadow and realized then what had happened to the other invaders.

From within the smoke and wreckage of the nearby buildings, other warriors, their dark skin and bright eyes identifying them as Krokans, had joined the fight.

They darted in and out of the chaos and speared the Orau from behind, the heart-shaped blades of their weapons tearing through the invaders' armor as if it were paper.

Blood sprayed as the Krokans yanked their blades free and turned them on other Orau. Bodies dropped one after another.

Reynolds snarled, wanting more of the action.

He shot forward again, noting the damage to his android form but ignoring it, and launched himself at the Orau who'd attacked and cornered him and his crew.

He killed three with as many shots, then emptied his weapon into a fourth before grabbing another gun that had been discarded by a dead soldier.

But as he went to re-engage, Reynolds realized that most, if not all, of the Orau invaders were already dead.

He saw two more fall in as many heartbeats, then a third, their killers' angry shadows appearing and disappearing with surgical precision.

The helpful Krokans began to slip away as mysteriously as they had appeared, leaving Reynolds standing in the middle of the road surrounded by the corpses of Orau invaders.

His crew and Sergeant Gib ran up behind him. Jiya stared after the shadows as they departed.

"Are you okay?" Jiya asked as Geroux looked him over.

"I'm fine," he muttered, brushing them off.

As much as he appreciated their concern, he had too many questions to worry about the condition of his android body. He needed to get his crew to safety before the tables turned anew.

Reynolds spun, grabbing Sergeant Gib by the shoulder. "Lead us to this shelter," he ordered.

The sergeant nodded, a true soldier, and started off, not even questioning the fact that he didn't work for Reynolds.

The crew and Reynolds chased after him.

A block or two later, Jiya realized that Maddox wasn't with them. She stuttered to a halt and made to turn around and race back.

"Where's Maddox," she called over the comm.

Reynolds grabbed her by the arm to stop her, pulling her with him.

"We can't leave him behi—"

"I'm good, Jiya," Maddox answered over the line. "Took the opportunity to cloak and slip off to do some recon now that everyone is safe."

Jiya growled and shook loose of Reynolds' grasp. "I wish someone would tell me shit before it happens."

Reynolds shrugged. "I didn't know he was going to do it either. I only realized he had when you turned back to find him."

"Not cool," Jiya muttered, then started off after the sergeant again.

Reynolds followed her.

He hadn't issued an order for Maddox to run off like that, but it made perfect sense, and Reynolds was kicking himself because he hadn't thought of it.

Fortunately, the general was trained for this type of situation, unlike the rest of the crew, so Reynolds trusted the general to operate on his own.

Now, if only Maddox could figure out what was going on, that'd be great.

But if he couldn't, Reynolds had an idea of his own.

He'd bust heads until people told him what he wanted to know.

CHAPTER EIGHT

Sergeant Gib led them to the shelter through back alleys and bombed-out streets.

Every step Jiya took made her stomach churn.

Although the majority of the Krokan people had managed to find shelter or get out of the line of fire, far too many hadn't.

Bodies littered the streets, and Jiya couldn't help but think that many of them had died simply because the SD *Reynolds* had shown up and taken a side.

She knew that was ridiculous, seeing as how the war had been going on forever by all accounts, but it didn't make her feel any better about her part in it.

Still, she was there now, and she wouldn't waste the opportunity to pay the Orau back for all they'd done to the Krokan people.

Her cheeks warmed as she imagined what she'd do to the bastards who had hurt so many people and destroyed so many innocent lives so they could raid the planet and move on once they were done.

It was so...so *vile*.

She didn't get a chance to imagine what else she wanted to do to the Orau scum because Sergeant Gib announced they were there.

Jiya looked up, blinking to focus, and stared as he led the crew down a dark, narrow alley.

Her paranoia rose up like dry tinder, and she pointed her gun at the sergeant's back as he walked ahead of them. She didn't like how easily she'd taken to killing, but she'd do anything to protect her crew.

If she had to kill the sergeant, she would without hesitation, and she'd worry about the consequences later.

No one would hurt her friends.

Fortunately, she didn't have to shoot Gib.

He led them to a brick wall at the end of the alley, shadows obscuring most everything there.

Jiya could see clearly thanks to her optics, but she still had no idea what Gib was doing, running them into a dead-end.

She realized things weren't as they seemed when he tapped out a code on a number of bricks in the wall and a section of it came open like a door.

"In here," he said, ushering them inside while staring down the alley to make sure no one saw them.

"You first, Ka'nak," Jiya ordered, and the warrior went in with his gun at the ready.

Reynolds followed, then Geroux, and Jiya brought up the rear. When she reached the door, she motioned Sergeant Gib in before her.

"I've got the door," she told him.

It was a test, of sorts, but Gib passed without issue.

He simply nodded and darted into the dark passage behind the others. Jiya shut the door behind them, and she sighed when she heard the sullen *thump* of its latch.

Then she chased after the others, a bit perturbed by the tight tunnel they were squeezed into, but that didn't last long.

A short while later, Gib opened another secret door in what appeared to be a random wall and led them into a great domed chamber. Voices struck her as soon as the door was opened, and she caught the scent of perfume and cologne and a variety of foods and beverages as she stepped into the room.

Her stomach grumbled.

"Fancy," Ka'nak remarked, retracting his helmet and staring at the crowd of people, all of whom had stopped what they were doing to stare back.

The Melowi warrior was right. The crowd looked as if they were at a ball or some social event far above Jiya's pay grade. Other than the obvious Krokan guards stationed about the room, everyone was dressed in fine clothing, and although she knew nothing about style, it was clear these outfits were at the top of the heap when it came to cost and fashion.

"Anyone else feeling a bit out of place?" Geroux asked, slipping behind Jiya so she wasn't being stared at directly.

It took a moment for the surprise of their arrival to wear off, then the people finally went back to what they were doing, although the conversation had dropped to a low murmur and didn't rise again.

"These are the elite of Krokus 4," Sergeant Gib explained, gesturing to the crowd milling about below them. "They come here or go to one of the other shelters when raids begin."

Jiya felt her cheeks warm. "And the regular people?" she asked, not expecting an answer.

Sergeant Gib shuffled his feet and Jiya could tell he didn't want to meet her eyes, but he did after an uncomfortable moment.

"I'm one of those regular people," he said quietly. "I don't get a say in who ends up here."

Jiya made ready to snap back, to argue, but the look on the sergeant's face told her he was telling the truth. He was just a soldier.

Another universal constant: there were always haves and have-nots.

She drew a deep breath and twisted her head to the side, popping her neck to rid it of some of her pent-up aggression and stiffness.

Geroux, realizing her mood, wrapped her arms around her friend and squeezed. Jiya leaned into the hug, glad to have Geroux there.

Reynolds came over and waved Sergeant Gib on.

"We're safe," he told her, thinking that perhaps she had been concerned about the crew and that was what she was reacting to.

That was part of it, of course, but not all of it.

Once more memories of her father and the life she'd led back on Lariest sprang to mind. This time, however, she didn't sweep them aside or hide from them.

She clung to them and embraced them.

They pissed her off, and she wanted to be pissed off.

Jiya glared down at the Krokus 4 elite, picturing her father and his advisors and business partners and visiting dignitaries, and she growled. She wanted to jump into the crowd and shriek and scream and punch and kick; teach each and every one of these elitist fools a lesson.

She only stopped herself when she realized she was acting just like them, deciding what was right and wrong for a whole class of people.

Her anger spilled from her like a deflated balloon.

"Why are we here?" she asked.

Sergeant Gib, who'd given her distance as Reynolds suggested, inched back over to answer her.

"President Jaer Pon and the vice president are here, and they wanted to meet with you," the sergeant answered. "I'm supposed to take you to them."

The sergeant turned and started off, but Jiya grabbed his arm.

"First, answer a question for me," she requested.

He nodded, unsure if he had an answer she wanted to hear.

"Who were those people who helped us back there?" she asked. "The ones who killed those Orau?"

Sergeant Gib sighed. "I don't know much," he replied, but Jiya knew he was lying.

"You mean you can't tell us much?" she countered.

He gave a noncommittal shrug and said nothing.

"They were Krokans," Reynolds stated, and Jiya saw the sergeant's face waver before he got his expression under control.

"They were different, though," Reynolds went on, probing. "They fought with spears and didn't wear armor, but they were definitely Krokans."

The sergeant said nothing for a moment, staring stone-faced between Reynolds and Jiya, and just when he appeared ready to crack and answer the question, the president's voice rang out over the crowd.

"There you are," he called, waving the crew and sergeant over. "I've been waiting for you."

The crowd quieted as the president insisted the crew come to him. The people obliged his wishes by moving to the side and making a path.

"We need to go," Sergeant Gib said, relieved to be off the hook.

Jiya fought the urge to yank him back by the scruff of his neck and demand he answer the question, but she knew it would cause nothing but trouble, especially with every eye in the place on her and the crew.

She snarled and started after the sergeant. Geroux clasped her hand as they walked, and she offered her friend the biggest smile she could muster.

It wasn't much, but Geroux knew she meant every crooked centimeter of it.

The crew made their way through the crowd. On their way to the president's side, Jiya was reminded once more that she needed to rein her temper in and get a complete view of things before she acted on her assumptions.

The elite might be dressed in fancy clothes and expensive outfits, but as she drew closer to them, she realized that they didn't look much better off than the people Jiya had passed in the streets.

Despite their wealth and influence, the elite of Krokus 4

looked every bit as tired as the soldiers and the gardeners and the cooks she'd seen around the compound. Their cheeks were sunken and drawn and their skin seemed pale up close, its deep ebony lacking in luster.

She started to feel bad about jumping to conclusions, but she couldn't bring herself to apologize, even if only in her head. She'd seen too many elitists who were exactly what she'd classified them as.

Just because these people had suffered too, they weren't any better than those who had been left behind in the streets to die.

She straightened as she strode past them, hand in hand with Geroux, and met every gaze that looked her way, staring until they turned away.

It was petty, yeah, but it gave her a sense of satisfaction.

The sergeant led them up a flight of steps to a small landing separated from the crowd. Dozens of guards surrounded it, and Jiya spotted the president, the vice president, and the minister gathered near the center.

The vice president shuffled as if she were nervous.

"Thank you for coming," Jaer Pon said once they had come to stand before him.

Jiya bit back her snarky reply of, "As if we had a choice."

Reynolds stepped forward to keep her from exploding.

"As you see, there is far more to our situation than the Orau invaders attacking us in space," Jaer Pon stated. "They have become increasingly more dangerous, raiding our land and killing our people. And as you have observed, there is little we can do once they begin their bombardments."

"It takes nearly all our resources to maintain the dome

and keep it from collapsing under the assault," Vice President Shal Ura added. "Our destroyers do what they can, shooting down the missiles and invading troop carriers, but the Orau overwhelm them, making it impossible to deflect even a small part of the threat."

"We need your technology," Jaer Pon stated bluntly, no longer worried about pretense. "But in actuality, we need more than just your technology," he clarified. "We need your help to end this."

The vice president stiffened as if surprised by the president's statement. She glanced at him, narrowed eyes uncertain.

"We'd be glad to help," Reynolds replied without hesitation, "but I'm not certain what we can do to help you beyond advance your defensive technology."

"You can do what we cannot," the president went on. "You can take the fight to the Orau, whereas we are stuck on the defensive, unable to send our small fleet after the source of the attacks without leaving ourselves defenseless."

"You want us to fight your war for you?" Ka'nak asked.

Jiya knew the thought excited the Melowi warrior, but she'd asked the same question in her head—only *her* tone was one of disgust that he would ask them for that.

"I don't think—" Jiya started, but Reynolds silenced her with a glance, his eyes steely.

"What are you suggesting, Mister President?" Reynolds asked.

"Yes, *what* are you suggesting?" Shal Ura repeated, obviously frustrated by the direction of the conversation. "We cannot involve these people in our battles, Jaer Pon," she argued.

The president shook his head, dismissing her. "They want to negotiate, let us negotiate. What say you, Reynolds? Do you want the technology for the filtration system? What about some of our other tech? We have more than you've seen. Much more," the president teased.

Are we seriously considering this? Jiya asked over the link.

Let's get a clear view of what he wants before we reject it out of hand, Reynolds shot back.

Out of hand? she growled. *This whole situation is* already *out of hand. We should pack up and leave, fire the ESD at the Orau assholes, and get the fuck out of the galaxy.*

I suspect that's what the president is suggesting, Reynolds told her. *At least some part of that, mostly the ESD part.*

Jiya huffed but shut up, letting Reynolds negotiate with the president without her in his ear.

"What exactly do you want us to do, Mister President?" Reynolds questioned, demanding a straight answer.

"In exchange for all of our technical data, a sanctuary, and supplies, we want the schematics to this defensive ring of yours, but we also want you to take the fight to the Orau in our stead."

"You realize we don't have a standing army?" Reynolds asked.

"You won't need one," the president argued. "The Orau are a nomadic people. Their outposts are little more than collections of huts and tents. Their true threat lies in their ships and artillery."

"They bombard us from long range, and there is nothing we can do to stop them. However, there is much that *you* can do. A single salvo from your ship to their launchers would set them back years. It would give us a chance to recover, to repair and assemble this defensive ring. We could protect ourselves."

"Jaer Pon!" the vice president cried, covering her mouth with her hand to hide her frustration at his demands.

Jiya glanced at Reynolds, and she could see he was contemplating it.

Her first thought was to argue against it again, thinking much like the vice president was that it wasn't their battle and getting involved put the crew and the ship at risk.

Then she realized how easily the *Reynolds* had swatted the Orau ships when they'd first arrived.

While the Orau posed a huge threat to the crew here on Krokus 4, once inside the superdreadnought, there was likely little the Orau could do to them.

They could pummel the bastards with near impunity from space and do to them what they had been doing to the Krokans all these years.

The thought brought a smile to her face.

"This is preposterous, Jaer Pon," Vice President Shal Ura exclaimed, shaking her head. "We cannot do this."

"We accept," Reynolds stated, overriding the vice president's defiance. She gasped.

"You will do this for us?" Jaer Pon asked as if unsure he'd heard the AI correctly.

"We will, in exchange for the data on your filtration system, safe haven for future visits, and supplies as needed. We don't need the rest of your tech."

Jaer Pon grinned at that and stuck his hand out. "We have a deal, then," he agreed, excitement clear in his voice.

"My minister here, To Gul, will provide you with the coordinates of the most dangerous of the Orau installations. Once you have rained fire down upon them, we will gladly provide you with the tech specifications you need in exchange for those of the defensive ring."

Reynolds nodded. "Fair enough."

President Jaer Pon grinned and grabbed the minister by his shoulder. "Come, To Gul, we have much to prepare," he told the older male. To Reynolds, he said, "We will transmit the information to your ship posthaste."

Jaer Pon and his advisor raced off before anyone could argue.

Once they were gone, Vice President Shal Ura sighed and wished the crew luck, turning around and stomping off without another word.

"We're really going after these guys?" Geroux asked.

"Looks like we are," Jiya answered.

"We are," Reynolds confirmed. "Doing so serves two purposes. We get the tech we wanted, and we get to see the Orau up close and personal."

"And that's a good thing?" Geroux asked.

"Given that they, like the Loranians, have been influenced by the Kurtherians, I believe it is," he answered. "After we left here, I would have directed that we hunt down the Orau anyway. This gives us a better reason for it than simple curiosity."

"Bloodshed and ass-kicking!" Ka'nak shouted.

"There will be plenty of that," Reynolds assured the Melowi.

Jiya nodded, agreeing to go.

Whatever she thought about the president and his

elitist supporters, she'd be doing this for the rank-and-file people on the streets, those who'd lost loved ones and friends in today's bombardment and invasion as well as all the others.

"Let's do this," she said with a growl. "I have a new armored boot I need to break off in someone's ass."

CHAPTER NINE

Maddox stood outside the servants' entrance to the presidential compound, hiding in a mass of overly thick foliage to keep from burning out his unperfected cloaking device.

He had circled around the compound after the bombardment had ceased, taking advantage of the empty streets and black smoke that obscured most of the city.

He'd kept tabs on the crew over the comm, listening in as they went to meet with the president, but he'd maintained radio silence since assuring Jiya that he was okay.

He didn't want to accidentally give away his location or his plans in case someone was capable of listening in on the comm frequency.

Maddox grinned as he hunkered in the bushes, waiting, watching. Stalking.

He missed the old days before he'd become a general, before he'd been betrayed by Lemaire and locked away to rot.

Now, out here on his own, just his wits and skills to

serve him, he felt freer than ever before, even after Jiya had helped him escape from her father's prison.

He had staked out the servants' entrance as soon as he could reach it, but he was worried that Kah Dur had already left the compound or been killed in the Orau onslaught.

A number of servants had left since he'd arrived—since the attack ended—but he hadn't seen or heard anything about Kah Dur.

He wondered if he were wasting his time and whether he should rejoin Reynolds and the crew. They wouldn't be hard to track down. He hadn't heard what arrangements they'd made with the president, although he'd determined what they were doing from Jiya's outburst.

Maddox was sure Reynolds wouldn't make a bad deal. The crew would do what they had to for the betterment of the ship, the crew, and the mission. He had decided that he could contribute best by getting the information they needed.

It had been so long since he'd been on a mission that didn't involve a ship or an army that he'd nearly forgotten the joy of being out on his own, with only himself to rely on.

That wasn't entirely true, of course. He had the crew and the power of a superdreadnought in orbit, but down here, he was alone. He never realized how much he missed that feeling.

As much as he loved being part of a good crew, there was nothing in that which satisfied the adventurer in him. To stand toe to toe with adversity was a pleasure he could never describe.

And although he would never leave his crew, he needed this right now.

He sat and waited and watched, unable to wipe the smile from his face. It wasn't until he spotted Kah Dur slipping from the entrance and angling along the wall of the compound that the general turned serious and put on his war face.

Maddox triggered the cloaking device and trailed Kah Dur, staying close enough to ensure the servant couldn't slip away but far enough back that there was no chance that she would notice him, even if he weren't cloaked.

She walked through the wreckage of the city as if it were just another day, her eyes on the ground, never once looking at the destruction surrounding her. Maddox wondered if that was how the people here survived or if this was simply who she was.

There was a fine line between callous and numb, and Maddox couldn't tell which side Kah Dur was on.

She strode on a for a long time, winding her way through the almost deathly silent city until Maddox found himself in the same area where they'd been ambushed by the Orau earlier.

Kah Dur splashed through the same puddles Maddox had waded through hours earlier, and she marched past the bodies littering the streets and sidewalks. She didn't look at the corpses or the guns or any of it. She simply walked on.

After a short while, she left the worst of the aftermath of the attack behind, although it was clear from the area of town they were now entering that it had seen its own share of battles.

While none of the damage was fresh, time having left its mark on the ruins, there wasn't much to differentiate this part of town from the one that had just been bombed.

The buildings were old and decrepit. A gray pallor seemed to hang over the streets.

It hung over the people, too.

Citizens were going about their business in the streets as if Ocelora hadn't been bombarded only hours before.

Kah Dur avoided the others, keeping her head down as she had the entire way. The locals seemed inclined to do the same, avoiding eye contact or any appearance of noticing anyone else.

Maddox slipped past the people, avoiding them as best he could to keep from alerting them that someone they couldn't see shared the streets with them.

It was easy with as few of them as were out.

Maddox began to become disillusioned as the servant continued on, never stopping or looking around, never seeming to reach her destination. She walked on and on without looking up or examining landmarks or even widening the narrow slits of her eyes.

It wasn't until the streets were empty and the lights that illuminated the city had nearly all failed and fallen dark in their floating orbs above that she slowed and looked around.

Maddox felt adrenaline surge through him as she cast furtive glances every which way, then darted down an almost invisible alley off the street she'd been traveling.

He followed her without hesitation, knowing that even if he were directly behind her, she wouldn't be able to see through Takal's wondrous cloaking device.

Maddox grinned as he followed her through the darkness, only to catch her slipping into a crevice in the wall near the center of the alley.

He went over and examined it, glad to see that it was wide enough for him to fit through despite his armor. Before he did, though, he listened to make sure she hadn't stopped on the other side. When he heard her soft footsteps heading away, he eased through the crevice and followed her into deeper darkness.

Once he'd gotten close enough to see her again, he moved behind her silently. He was glad when she came to a halt at last.

She looked around with her bright eyes once again, then stepped through a tattered door that was cracked open. Maddox could hear voices inside; soft, whispering voices.

He eased up to the door after making certain no one stood watch, then crept inside the decrepit building Kah Dur had gone into. A flicker of candlelight and shadow drew him in deeper. The voices called to him.

"What say you, Kah Dur?" someone asked in a muffled voice Maddox could barely hear.

Maddox wanted to follow her, to get closer so he could hear better, but the pathway she'd chosen was little more than a crack in the wreckage of the building. It was littered with debris and rotted wood.

Attempting to move across it in his armored boots would make too much noise, alerting the clandestine congregation that he was there.

He didn't want that.

So, he remained where he was and strained to hear

what was said, reminding himself to have Takal increase the sensory input of the suit beyond just vision.

"I left as soon as I could," he heard her answer. "The attack…me."

Maddox growled under his breath as he realized she and the people she'd come all this way to meet were moving away from the entrance. If they went farther, he would either lose track of them entirely or be forced to follow after them and risk being heard.

"…Pon," he heard a masculine voice mutter. "Still alive?"

Maddox stiffened at hearing that.

What are you planning, Kah Dur?

"…the compound…chambers…still."

Maddox only caught part of the servant's reply and he edged forward, getting as close as he could without making a sound.

It wasn't much help.

"…kill…" he heard a different male state, the venom in his voice clearer than anything he said.

"Yes," someone else said. "We must."

Maddox realized then that the voices were becoming clearer.

He shifted away from the cluttered entrance as their voices got louder, obviously headed back in his direction.

"We have no choice," the first person said. "The master wishes it so, and thus it shall be."

Maddox eased as far to the side of the entryway as he possibly could and held his breath despite knowing no one could hear it with his helmet on.

The servant scraped and crawled across the debris, and Maddox was glad he hadn't tried to sneak past since there was no way he could have done it silently. The light, slim servant crunched and stomped her way back through the trash as if a herd of wild animals trailed her.

She stood up once she cleared it and brushed the dirt from her uniform, cast a quick glance behind her, and left the building without a word.

The males behind her stopped at the far end of the clutter.

Maddox leaned around the corner to take a better look, still cloaked.

What he saw surprised him.

The two people Kah Dur had been speaking to were dressed in dark robes, looking like religious disciples. He could see by their skin color and eyes that they were Krokans, but there was nothing about either that would make them stand out in a crowd of their people.

He memorized their faces as best he could in case he needed to recall them, but they didn't remain still for long.

They gazed after Kah Dur for a moment, even though she was long gone by then, then turned back to one another.

"I'll prepare the acolytes," one said. The other only nodded.

A moment later, both males made their way across the debris path, following the servant. Maddox eased back and let them pass.

He had a pretty good idea Kah Dur would return to the compound, so he let her leave without tracking her, but those two were a mystery to him.

They stepped out into the dark alley and made their way to the street, strolling casually, as if they hadn't just been making threats against the president, which was what Maddox believed.

He had heard Jaer Pon's name mentioned, and it made sense that these people were plotting to kill the president of Krokus 4, especially after what Kah Dur had told the crew earlier.

Perhaps that was what she had really been warning them about—her attempt to have the president killed while they were at the compound.

Maybe she'd meant to protect the crew from any backlash, knowing the room was bugged and being observed. If the crew were clearly visible on the holos, nothing would implicate them.

But that was not how things worked out.

The attack had pulled them from their guest chambers out onto the street where no one except Sergeant Gib could attest to their whereabouts.

Maddox sighed as he chased the acolytes, staying close to them as they drifted in the general direction of the compound.

Maddox decided that if they were plotting to kill the president while the crew was still on the planet, then it was his duty to stop them.

At the very least, he would follow them and see what they were up to.

CHAPTER TEN

Back aboard the SD *Reynolds*, the crew made arrangements to strike the Orau settlement on Krokus 1, where the minister had directed them.

"What about Maddox?" Jiya asked once they were back on the bridge, not liking how things were playing out. "We're not just going to leave him on the planet while we go bomb another one, are we?"

"Maddox is fine, Jiya," Reynolds assured her. "He is tracking down the servant who warned us about the president and working to discover what her motivations are."

"Probably that President Jaer Pon is an asshole and we can't trust him," she stated, making a face. "As much as I want to go and blow these Orau assholes up, it still feels to me as if we're being used."

"Of course we are," Reynolds replied with a shrug. "That's politics."

"But not ours," she pressed.

"No, maybe not, but I don't see anything we're doing

here as a bad thing," he told her. "After what the Orau did to the people of Krokus 4, they deserve to get their dicks kicked in, don't you think?"

"Absolutely!" Jiya answered. "But however good this is going to feel, what are we opening ourselves up to?"

"The joy of stomping the skulls of murderous morons?" Ka'nak suggested.

"I'm all for that," Tactical called. "I get firsties!"

Jiya sighed. "It's like talking to walls," she muttered. "Dumb walls."

Asya shrugged. "I get what you're saying, Jiya, but I do not really see a downside to taking out a bunch of assholes who are killing innocents." She gestured to the viewscreen. "I recorded the attack on the planet from up here. It was brutal. I could play it for you if you want."

Jiya shook her head. "No thanks, I was there. Not up to re-living it, even if it's from another perspective."

"Then I'm not sure what the problem is," Asya pressed.

"I think it's that I just don't want to be used by that piece-of-shit president," she shot back.

"Is this about your dad?" Geroux asked quietly.

Jiya snarled. "No. Yes. Maybe. Fuck if I know, but now that you mention it, this does feel like I'm working for my father to keep the peasants in line by a show of force."

"But it's not the Krokans who are being taught a lesson here," Ka'nak argued.

"You sure about that?" Jiya asked the warrior. "Here we are, the most potent force in the system, and we're working for a jackass like Jaer Pon," she said. "No matter how you twist things, it looks like we're servants doing his bidding. Watch us punish the Orau, which, again, I'm okay with, but when you ask the people of Krokus 4 who did it, I guarantee they'll say their president did."

"So this is about your ego?" Ka'nak asked.

Jiya shook her head slowly. The corners of her mouth curled up into a weak smile. "Yes, Ka'nak, this is all about my ego. Fuck the Krokans, fuck the Orau, and fuck everyone else for having an opinion. I just want people to know it was me, and me alone, who kicked the Orau's asses."

"Why didn't you just say so?" Ka'nak wondered. "That's something I can relate to."

Jiya growled and mimed choking the Melowi warrior. "One of these days."

"I understand your concerns, Jiya," Reynolds said, "but selfishly, I think it's best for everyone if we end the Orau threat. Then we can look into the Etheric signature without interference. We can't get the information we need to continue our mission until the fighting ends."

Jiya gave him a thumbs-up, tired of trying to explain herself. "Then let's get to it, Captain," she said, going over and dropping into the seat at her console. The thought of the no-win mission cast a darkness over her that she couldn't shake off.

Reynolds took that as a sign to get underway. "Ensign Alcott, do you have the coordinates for the Orau base on Krokus 1 locked in?"

"Yes, sir," Ria answered. "Locked, and the Gate drive is cycling. We're ready to go at your command."

Reynolds grinned. "Why can't the rest of you be like Ensign Alcott?"

"Because I couldn't possibly get my nose that far up your ass, Reynolds," Tactical answered.

"Hey!" Ria argued. "That's not nice."

"Have you *met* Tactical?" Asya asked, laughing.

"Never mind all this." Reynolds sighed. "Let's go kick some alien ass."

"Opening the Gate now," Ria informed.

"Let's hit it," Reynolds ordered.

The SD *Reynolds* started forward, sliding easily through the Gate, the portal sealing behind them.

A few moments later, they appeared on the far side of Krokus 1 where they'd been told the Orau outpost was located.

"We're here, sir," Ria announced.

Reynolds watched without comment and ordered, "Report."

"It looks as if the coordinates and intel your buddy Jaer Pon provided were accurate," Jiya replied. "There is an outpost nestled in a mountain valley on the other side of the planet. I'm detecting a large amount of firepower, as well as... Oh, you have *got* to be fucking kidding me," she exclaimed.

"What is it?" Reynolds asked, turning to look at the first officer.

"No wonder Jaer Pon sent us here," Jiya muttered. "This planet is inhabited."

"Uh, yeah," Tactical said. "By the fucking enemy."

"Obviously," Jiya shot back, "but unless these nomadic twatwhistles brought their entire planet with them, there is no way all the lifeforms I'm picking up down there are Orau."

"Let me see," Reynolds said, putting her console's data up on the main viewscreen. He snarled as it scrolled. "That ingrown prick," Reynolds growled.

"I'm owed an, 'I told you so,'" Jiya announced evenly while studying the data.

"Data is telling me that there are two distinct species down there," Asya clarified. "The first is definitely Orau, but the second is unknown to the system. They're likely the original inhabitants of the planet before the Orau showed up."

"And if they're still there with a bunch of cutthroat pirates, my guess is that they are being used for something illicit and unkind," Jiya said.

"Slaves, most likely." Reynolds growled at the realization that things weren't going to be as easy as they'd expected.

"Even more reason to blow these fuckers to ass dust," Tactical argued.

"Maybe, but the plan was to surveil the outpost and *then* blow it the fuck up," Reynolds replied. "It's not like we can do that now, not with a bunch of innocents in the way."

"Fuck it, I'm using it now!" Jiya said, throwing her hands up. "I told you so!" she shouted. "The presidential shitstain *knew* there were other people here when he sent us. He wants us to do his dirty work. If we're the ones killing all the locals, he can't be blamed for it. No political stink on his hands."

"And here we agreed to do just that," Asya added, grinning as she stared at Reynolds, watching for his reaction. "Just like Jiya said."

"I'm not finding any of this amusing," Reynolds said, looking over the data once again.

"What do you want us to do, *Captain*?" Jiya asked.

"Give me a minute," Reynolds barked, rubbing his metallic face as if that might actually do something.

"Don't really have a minute anymore," XO informed.

"What is it now?" Reynolds asked.

"Our little friend just Gated in on the other side of the planet," XO announced.

"Our friend? The Loranian ship?" Reynolds asked, spinning to XO's station for clarification. "Show me!"

The viewscreen flickered and zoomed in, and there in orbit above Krokus 1 sat the same Loranian ship that had attacked the SD *Reynolds* above Grindlevik 3.

"Those sons of weasel fuckers," Tactical blurted. "I'm warming up the Eat Shit and Die. I don't care what you say."

"Belay that," Reynolds shouted.

"Blow this," Tactical fired back.

"Silence! Now that the Loranian ship is here, we can't just stroll over there and start taking shots at the planet," Asya said.

"No, but we can start taking shots at those Loranian slug-fuckers," Tactical argued.

"Then we'd be engaging both them and the Orau, who'd no doubt join the Loranians in trying to blow holes in us." Reynolds sighed. "Things are always complicated when it comes to living beings."

"That's because you let Bethany Anne give you a damn conscience when it comes to meatbags, Reynolds," Tactical told him. "Stow that shit for a while, and you'll realize I'm right. We should just raze the planet and then park our railguns up that alien ship's rectum."

"The place is already razed," Asya informed them. "These Orau laid waste to the planet while gouging for resources, it looks like."

"You're not trying very hard to talk me out of this," Tactical warned.

"We're not nuking the planet, and that's final," Reynolds snarled.

"You take all the fun out of annihilation," Tactical told him.

"We've got movement at the ship," Asya reported. "There's a shuttle disembarking right now. It's headed to the surface."

"Lifeforms aboard?" Reynolds questioned.

"I'm picking up five distinct beings," Asya reported.

"If you were looking for a reason to agree with me," Tactical said, "this is it. This is the perfect opportunity, presenting itself on a golden fucking platter."

"I don't want anyone to remember this moment, but I agree with Tactical," Jiya announced, cringing as she said it. "We've got a chance to grab some of those Loranian pricks —no offense, Asya—and find out what the hell they want with us."

Asya shrugged off the comment.

"How do you propose we do that?" Reynolds asked.

"We pile into a cloaked shuttle and follow them down," Jiya suggested. "Find out where they're headed and what they're up to on the planet, then we use our boots as suppositories and figure out who they are and why they're following us."

"That's the best plan I've heard since my own," Tactical exclaimed. "I'm on Team Hemorrhoid over there."

Reynolds stood there silently for a moment, mulling his options, and it didn't take him long to decide. "Let's do it," he decided. "You, me, Ka'nak, Geroux, and San Roche will head down to the planet to find out what we can and try to capture these fucks for interrogation."

"What do you want us to do?" Asya asked.

"What Tactical wants," Reynolds replied.

"I'm not sure that's what we want to do, Reynolds," she told him.

"I mean, take the superdreadnought around the other side of the planet and start giving it to the Loranian ship."

"Really?" Asya asked.

"Really?" Tactical asked an instant later, no less surprised than Asya was.

"With some of their crew on the planet, maybe you can get them to sit still long enough to do real damage," Reynolds said.

"And if the Orau join the fight like you said earlier?" Asya asked.

"Blow them the fuck up too," Reynolds ordered. "Cry havoc and let slip the dogs of war!"

"Can't we just use guns like normal people?" Asya questioned. "Dogs in space do not make for a solid tactical strategy, not even on this ship."

"Throw the head at them if you need to," Reynolds told her. "Just make sure you hurt those pricks."

Asya grinned, snapping a salute.

Reynolds left the bridge, and Jiya followed him, waving Geroux and Ka'nak after her.

"Reach out to San Roche and have him meet us in the hangar bay, Asya," Jiya called back as she raced off the bridge.

She smiled as she did.

She couldn't help herself.

The fates were aligning, and both the opportunity to take a shot at the Loranian ship and its crew felt like an early Conception Day present.

She was going to have a ton of fun ripping this one open.

"The shuttle is free of the hangar bay," Ria reported.

Asya nodded, gesturing to Tactical's station. "Then it looks like it's time to go stir shit up."

"You're speaking my language," Tactical replied.

"Slowly and incoherently, with a lot of cussing?" Ria asked.

Tactical chuckled. "We might make a soldier of you yet."

"Get ready to open a Gate next to that piece-of-shit cruiser parading around as a Loranian ship," Asya ordered, "but do it carefully. I don't want them realizing we're coming until it's too late."

"Yes, sir," Ria replied, fingers flying over her console. "Gate opening in three…two…now."

"Go!" Asya ordered.

The SD *Reynolds* shot forward at the command, slipping into the portal and sliding through, transported almost immediately to the other side of Krokus 1. Like before, they appeared above and behind the Loranian ship.

Tactical unleashed his railguns with brutal efficiency.

The Loranian cruiser took nearly the full brunt of the blasts, bringing its shields up at the last second to deflect only a small measure of the attack.

Debris and atmosphere spewed from holes in the hull along the scorched aft quadrant of the ship near its engines. The ship listed and the crew of the SD *Reynolds* cheered, but their joy was short-lived.

The Loranian craft righted itself a moment later and swung about, bringing its own guns to bear.

"That is one tough motherfucker," Tactical admitted, although it was clear he hated saying it.

Return fire crashed into the SD *Reynolds'* gravitic shields, shaking the ship even as it withstood the barrage.

"I'm spooling up the ESD. I don't care what anyone says," Tactical announced.

Asya didn't bother to argue. She didn't figure the Loranian cruiser would stick around long enough for the device to power up and be used, but she could hope that it would.

"Orau fighter-bombers inbound," Ria reported.

"That was fast," Asya grumbled.

"I'm picking up six of them. No, make that eight," Ria corrected.

"It's going to get crowded up here real soon, folks, so let's do what we can to kick this fucker's ass before his friends arrive," Asya called.

Tactical hadn't stopped firing.

Back and forth the two ships went at each other, and although the SD *Reynolds* had gotten the better of the first exchange, it was clear the Loranian ship had been designed to take a beating and dish one out in return.

Its shields held as the railguns pounded them, the weapons only managing to punch through a few times, scoring hits on the hull and leaving scorch marks and warped steel behind.

Unfortunately, the same could be said for the *Reynolds*.

While their gravitic shields deflected most of the Loranian's attacks, enough of them got through to do real harm.

Asya kept the ship angled to avoid getting hit in the already damaged section of the hull, which ensured there was no loss of life aboard the ship, but it hadn't much helped to avoid sustaining new wounds.

Red lights gleamed across the bridge, and although Asya had muted the alarms, those from the lower decks reverberated under her feet.

"This is what a stalemate looks like," Tactical complained. "I'm not liking it much."

"Me either," Asya agreed. "We need to be smarter and stop going at these people head-on. We're not getting anywhere."

"Things are about to get worse," Ria announced. "The Orau are flanking us."

"Fuck a two-headed gralflie," Asya cursed. "Bring us up above the Loranian craft, Ria. Try to put their fat ass between us and the Orau ships."

"You realize the cruiser will adjust and move with us, right?" Tactical asked.

"As long as we get a few extra seconds out of it, that's fine," Asya fired back. "I'm buying time."

"Time to do what?" XO asked. "The ESD is still charging."

"To strip-mine their shields," she replied. "Hit it, Takal," she ordered over the comm.

As the SD *Reynolds* rose above the Loranian cruiser, the inventor fired a handful of cloaked proximity mines out of the trash chute at the ship below.

The cruiser immediately began to turn to avoid the encroaching superdreadnought, but unable to detect the mines, it turned directly into them.

A line of explosions rippled across the Loranian's shields. There was a flicker of energy, and then two of the mines struck the port side of the cruiser. Blasts of energy erupted as each collided with the hull.

The Loranian ship shuddered under the assault, the force of the blasts spinning the ship about. Its engines flared, and the craft spun out of control.

"Pound the grease out of that ship," Asya ordered, blood searing through her veins on a wave of adrenaline. "Take them out."

Tactical let loose with the railguns again, ripping great gouges in the side of the Loranian ship until its shields flickered to life again and deflected their ferocity.

The SD *Reynolds* trembled and Asya clasped at the arms of her chair to remain seated.

"The Orau are on us," Ria announced.

"Of course they are," Asya spat, but her blood was boiling. She wanted the Loranian ship mounted on her wall. "Stay on the cruiser," she ordered.

If there was a chance to put an end to this, now was it.

"Hit it with the ESD!" Asya screamed.

CHAPTER ELEVEN

Maddox followed the mysterious acolytes through Ocelora, wondering the entire time if he had heard them correctly back at the ramshackle building.

They led him to a quaint part of town where there was little damage from the Orau raids. Not to say there was none, but it was hardly at the level of much of the rest of the underwater city.

It mostly had smaller buildings, and Maddox thought that may have played a factor in its escaping the rampant damage that had happened elsewhere.

In the shadow of the larger buildings surrounding it, the area was in a valley within the city, out of the direct line of fire of the planet from which the Orau launched their attacks.

It made him wonder just why more people hadn't made their way there.

As it was there were few people on the streets, none of whom made any effort to examine or even look at the two acolytes as they walked by, much like the other passersby had done with Kah Dur, the servant.

Apparently, that's just how it is here, he thought.

The two strolled along without a care, finally arriving at what appeared to be a small home on the edge of the neighborhood.

The building looked indistinct and plain, and nothing about it spoke of anything nefarious.

Which made it perfect for two murderous acolytes to visit.

They walked to the door and knocked, being let in a moment later by an older female Maddox thought he remembered from when the servants had brought them the carts of food.

He eased closer to the house once the pair were inside and the door was closed again. As much as he wanted to kick the door in and go after the acolytes, he was certain there was more than just the one female in there with them.

Besides, kicking in the door wouldn't tell him what their plans were or what they intended to do next.

He fought his instinct to barge in and waited.

Fortunately, it didn't take long before the door opened again.

Maddox watched from across the street, still cloaked, as the two acolytes exited the house, although they no longer wore their robes.

Instead, they were dressed in suits of dark-blue powered armor and carried their helmets under their arms. The person who had let them in came out next, dressed the same way. A dozen more soldiers filed out after a moment, sealing the door behind them.

A hovercraft pulled up in front of the house and the small group piled into it, the vehicle rocking as it adjusted to accommodate their armored weight.

Maddox cursed under his breath.

As much as he wanted to take these militants down on his own, he knew better. Instead, he reached out over the comm to the SD *Reynolds*.

The silence that came back unnerved him.

Shit!

He tried again with the same results.

Then the vehicle started off, and Maddox knew he didn't have time to wait for anyone else to back him up.

Still, he knew better than to take on the vehicle and its occupants with the minimal equipment he had.

Carrying nothing more than a pistol, he was ill-equipped to take down a couple of soldiers, let alone an armored squad.

Rather than be stupid, he followed the vehicle. If he were right about what they intended from the snippet of conversation he'd overhead, he knew there'd be an army to stand against these soldiers once they arrived.

And if he were wrong, he'd worry about that when they got there. He focused at running full speed in the hovercraft's wake, hoping the power surge wouldn't degrade the cloak. The longer he stayed invisible, the greater the chance that the cloak would fail and he'd be seen.

Sometimes being right didn't make it better. It brought him no comfort when the vehicle parked a short distance from the presidential compound and the soldiers exited, piling up on the deserted street,

Maddox realized then why the acolytes and the others had chosen now to invade the compound.

In the wake of the bombing, all the guards who had been stationed on the walls were absent, likely tasked with protecting the president and the elites in the hidden bunker.

That meant security in the compound was at its weakest.

The soldiers donned their helmets and headed toward the servants' entrance Maddox had seen Kah Dur leave from, and it struck him that he hadn't seen a single guard the entire time he'd crouched in the bushes outside it.

That meant the would-be assassins would have direct access to the compound without having to battle their way in.

"Damn it!"

He needed to stop them *before* they got inside if he were going to avert a massacre.

Then it struck him.

Why the hell are they hitting the place now?

He'd already determined that the guards were at their lightest, stationed elsewhere, but he'd just realized that the situation gave them easier access but also robbed them of all their targets.

No guards meant no one *to* guard.

Maddox stumbled to a halt as the soldiers filed inside the servants' entrance, disappearing from sight.

"What the hell could they want?" he asked himself.

Does it matter? he answered.

If they had gathered in their safehouse, armored up, and driven here, they had to have a plan. There had to be a reason for it.

Rather than sit outside wondering, Maddox checked to make sure he was still cloaked and raced in after the squad of soldiers. There were a few servants in the halls once he was inside, but they didn't look any worse for wear.

Maddox ran down the hall, catching up to the soldiers before they'd gotten too far. They marched forward as if they belonged there, not expecting any challenges.

As it turned out, they were right.

Not a single guard approached them or activated an alarm as armed soldiers strolled through the nearly barren presidential palace. Maddox followed silently, wondering more and more what they were up to.

It wasn't until he recognized the path they were taking that it clicked.

Shit!

The soldiers passed an empty guard station at the end of the hall and made their way to a door in the middle of the corridor. They lined up outside, making ready, weapons raised, then one of the acolytes kicked the door open.

The squad of soldiers stormed the now-open room, weapons free and firing, filling the room with blaster fire.

It was the same guest chambers where the crew had stayed until the bombing.

Maddox growled low in his throat at seeing the soldiers piling into the room where he and the rest of the crew had been just hours before.

An uncomfortable thought slithered into his mind as he

listened to the destruction being wrought on the other side of the wall.

The acolytes hadn't come here to assassinate the president.

They'd been sent to kill Reynolds' crew.

CHAPTER TWELVE

On the surface of Krokus 1, the crew disembarked from the still-cloaked shuttle, leaving San Roche behind with orders similar to those that had been issued to L'Eliana: stay put, guard the shuttle, and be ready to provide support as needed.

On an unknown hostile planet, the crew would need all the support they could get.

The shuttle from the Loranian ship had landed a short distance ahead of them, and the crew had filed out and marched toward the ramshackle compound where the Orau had made their home since they'd taken over the planet.

Seeing the barren soil and dusty ground sickened Jiya as they left the shuttle behind and started after the Loranians. Dust kicked up in their wake, but she doubted anyone would notice. The steadily whipping wind made the place a brown swirl.

Jiya was spoiling for a fight as badly as she knew Ka'nak was.

Worried about the crew stuck on the SD *Reynolds*, reports of the battle with the Loranian cruiser and Orau fighter-bombers filtering down to them, she wanted this confrontation over so they could get back into space and rejoin the fight.

Still, she had a mission to accomplish and she'd finish it first, no matter how badly she wanted to take part in dismantling the Loranian cruiser that had been stalking them.

At least down here, there was a chance she could find out the information they wanted. All they had to do was capture one of the Loranians. Or all of them. She was indifferent to the total.

She wasn't much for torture, but that didn't stop her from imagining what would happen to the Loranians if the crew caught them alive.

A shudder ran through her at the thought, and she pushed it aside.

She wasn't a murderer, but she'd damn well do what was necessary to make sure none of her crew or any more innocents were hurt by the Orau, marauding slags that they were.

"They're not far ahead of us," Geroux reported, tracking the Loranian crew with a program she'd whipped up as soon as she climbed aboard the shuttle.

It wasn't exactly a tracker, seeing as how they hadn't been able to tag the Loranian crew. It functioned more like a predictive algorithm.

As Geroux explained it, the program accumulated the

local geography such as building locations, street layout, and the basic blueprints of the Orau outpost and ran it through the system, making a best guess as to where the crew might be headed.

Had they been in Ocelora or another large city the program would have been a waste of time, but since the outpost was simplistic and the nature of the larger buildings obvious, Geroux predicted the algorithm was ninety-eight percent accurate.

That was good enough for Jiya, even if she could have guessed where they were going without a program's aid.

She didn't care how they found the assholes as long as they did.

"I've got an idea," Reynolds said as they neared the Loranian shuttle, its hatch sealed against the nasty weather.

"Does it involve blowing something up?" Ka'nak asked, glancing at the shuttle.

"It does indeed," Reynolds replied, grinning.

"Then I'm in," Ka'nak announced. "Let's do this."

Jiya shrugged. She knew the shuttle was empty, all the crew having left it; that intel had been confirmed by the SD *Reynolds* and Asya before they engaged the Loranian cruiser. As such, it didn't hurt to make it harder for the Loranians to get back to their ship.

"How about we rig it and wait?" she suggested.

"Where's the fun in that?" Ka'nak asked.

"It's less fun but more prudent," she replied. "If we blow this thing up while we're chasing its crew they're going to know we're here, killing whatever surprise we've acquired by flying down here cloaked."

"Logic sucks," Ka'nak muttered.

"For sure, but Geroux will set it up so the explosives are on a trigger," Jiya explained. "I might even be able to convince her to let you push the button." She glanced at her friend.

"I guess." Geroux sighed, winking at Jiya when Ka'nak wasn't looking.

"Fine," he mumbled, stomping over to the shuttle, the crew in tow.

Reynolds handed him the explosives. "Don't use all the explosives, and don't blow yourself up either," he warned.

"The longer I hang around you people, the more I want to," he told them, dropping under the shuttle and crawling across the ground to find a good place to plant the explosives.

"I sometimes wonder if he's serious," Geroux stated.

"I keep saying we need to schedule psychiatric tests for the crew before we take them on," Jiya argued.

"Then there'd be an empty ship floating in space somewhere without a crew," Reynolds replied. "*Or* an AI," he added before the others could.

Geroux giggled and Jiya swallowed a laugh, stepping away to look down the road toward the outpost to make sure no one was watching them.

Nothing indicated they had been seen.

Still, she stood guard impatiently until Ka'nak was finished connecting the explosives and Geroux had synced them to her computer.

"Anytime we want, the shuttle goes boom," Geroux told them with a smile.

"Maybe we should wait until the crew returns and blast them then before we go home?" Ka'nak suggested.

"And miss out on capturing one of these assholes?" Jiya asked. "No fucking way. I want one of these guys alive."

"You going to be the one to interrogate him?" Ka'nak wondered.

She shrugged. "Probably not, but I will sure as hell watch and bet on how long he lasts."

"I'm starting to think I'm raising a crew of miscreants," Reynolds mused.

"We get it from you," Jiya fired back, chuckling. "A soldier is only as depraved as his command system."

"Which explains so damn much." Ka'nak laughed.

"Come on," Reynolds told them, cutting the banter off and ushering them down the makeshift road toward the outpost. "We need to get to these scumbags before they complete their dirtside mission, whatever that may be."

"I'm not sure it really matters since these guys aren't making it back to their ship," Ka'nak countered. "Even if they come back with more people or weapons or whatever, they're going boom the second they climb into that shuttle."

"As satisfying as that might be, it leaves too many questions hanging," Reynolds replied. "I'll gladly nuke them once we know what they hope to accomplish here, but I don't like not knowing what they're up to."

"Then let's stop chit-chatting and find these fucks," Jiya said, pressing ahead, her weapon out and at the ready.

She was dying to vent her anger on a living enemy.

A short distance down the road the opportunity presented itself.

Three Orau soldiers in dusty black and red armor stepped from one of the smaller huts near the edge of the outpost. They stumbled to a halt as they spied the crew advancing toward them. Their weapons whipped up immediately.

"So much for stealth." Reynolds sighed, firing on the Orau before they could shoot the crew.

Ka'nak and Jiya followed suit, blaster fire tearing through the dusty space between the two groups.

Unfortunately for the Orau marauders, the dust and dirt did nothing to protect them from the Federation weapons.

The three Orau fell beneath the onslaught. Each took several shots as they attempted to fight back, but their armor, worn and battered by the elements and past battles, failed them.

The Orau crumpled to the ground lifeless, smoking holes adding to the dust they'd kicked up in their death throes.

To Jiya's regret, their deaths didn't go unnoticed.

More Orau soldiers spilled from the various huts and tents in various states of undress, but almost every single one of them carried a weapon of some sort.

"Weapons *free*!" Reynolds shouted. "Highest body count gets a prize."

"Does friendly fire count?" Jiya asked through gritted teeth as she opened fire.

Ka'nak snorted, taking potshots at the surprised Orau soldiers as they tried to make sense of what was going on.

"Just thought I'd ask," Jiya added, standing shoulder to

shoulder with the Melowi warrior and pouring gunfire into the Orau.

Reynolds and Geroux joined them, the crew spreading across the dusty street to find whatever cover they could scare up.

Blaster fire shrieked all around, but the dust and the Orau lack of calibrated weapons and advanced optics distinctly gave the advantage to the crew of the SD *Reynolds*.

Jiya dropped a guy who staggered out of his tent without any pants. He raised his gun in her direction, the dangerous one, but he didn't manage to hit the trigger before Jiya blasted him in the gut.

He went down screaming.

So did a bunch of his companions.

The crew pressed forward, taking advantage of the surprise.

Soldier after soldier dropped in their wake, and when Jiya went to reload, she noticed the Loranian crew bolt from one of the bigger huts midway inside the compound.

Dozens of Orau marauders encircled them and ran alongside.

"Shit!" Jiya growled, seeing them fleeing. "There they are."

The crew went to give chase, but more of the Orau spilled from their holes, crawling into the light.

These, unlike the earlier ones, were fully armed and armored.

What had been a simple exercise of point and pull the trigger on an ill-equipped, unprepared foe had become a true battle.

A shot slammed into Jiya's chest and drove her back a step, and she was gladder than ever for Takal's upgrades to the Federation armor.

She slipped behind a hut to give herself a second to catch her breath, then she crouched and eased around the corner.

She sprayed the legs of the soldiers racing toward her, dropping them in screaming heaps in front of those behind them and slowing all of them down.

Still, as she looked out over the Orau soldiers coming toward her, she realized there were simply too many of them for the crew to take out like this.

"I'm thinking now would be a great time for artillery strikes," she called.

"Already on it," Reynolds replied.

And not more than a few seconds later, the San Roche-piloted shuttle appeared in the air above them. While limited in firepower, its simple weapons were far more effective than the handheld pistols the crew carried.

Death rained down on the Orau marauders as San Roche earned his keep as a new member of the crew.

"Was that what you needed?" San Roche asked through the comm.

The Orau scattered beneath the unexpected onslaught, racing for cover although they didn't completely abandon the fight.

"Perfect," Jiya called back, giving the shuttle pilot a thumbs-up. It was like the Telluride had found his niche.

San Roche strafed the ground, doing his best to clear the streets of Orau soldiers, and Jiya grimaced as she saw one of the nearby buildings collapse under the blasts of the shuttle's weapons.

Splinters and dust exploded into the air, the remnants of the makeshift building sparking before flames licked into the sky. Orau shrieked and ran. One was on fire and didn't make it far, flopping to the ground after a few steps. His corpse continued to burn.

"Go easy on the infrastructure, San Roche," Jiya warned, realizing the potential for collateral damage. "We know there are more than just Orau on Krokus 1, but we haven't seen any of the locals yet. We can't risk destroying buildings with innocents inside." *They have enough to worry about without us adding to it.*

San Roche muttered an affirmative and adjusted his fire, keeping it isolated on the Orau soldiers. Jiya understood she was limiting his effectiveness in the long run, but she'd much rather risk letting Orau get away than wantonly kill innocents.

"These guys aren't backing down," Ka'nak muttered, a hint of admiration in his voice.

"They're protecting the Loranians," Reynolds explained, gesturing down the street to where the Loranian shuttle occupants had fled within a protective cordon of Orau. "Whatever deal these guys have, it must be worth of a hell of a lot for the Orau to sacrifice their lives. We need to separate them and find out what they're up to."

"Clear a path so we can follow them," Jiya ordered San Roche, and the shuttle's sole occupant complied without hesitation.

A barrage of energy blasts ripped up the dirt street on the left and forced the Orau soldiers to retreat. Jiya and the others took advantage of the opening and shot out from behind cover, racing toward the nearest building close to the Loranians.

Orau soldiers cowered there as the crew skirted the corner.

The Orau barely knew what hit them.

Jiya turned the corner firing. The looks of shock on the supposed Vikings' faces immediately turned to those of agony and fear.

Ka'nak and Geroux joined Jiya in the attack, Reynolds appeared a second later after having taken out an Orau straggler who'd remained in the street nearby.

Jiya felt a blast clip her arm and she growled at the impact, letting the blow's momentum spin her around. She went with it, pivoting as if she'd meant to do that and then loosing a blast at the Orau who'd shot her.

He grimaced as he died, the smirk of his success forever frozen on his lips as he crumpled to the ground.

"We need to get on those Loranians before we lose them," Reynolds called, peeking around the corner while bursts of energy fire seared the air around him.

"You got eyes on the Loranians, San Roche?" Jiya asked over the comm.

San Roche came back a second later. "I do, but you have bigger issues headed your way," he replied.

"What does that mean?" Geroux asked.

"The Loranian host is stirring up the Orau," he answered. "There are about fifty soldiers massed behind the larger building on the left at the end of the street." San Roche paused a moment before coming back, "Now the Loranians are on the move, and there is no way I can attack either group without doing a bunch of damage to the surrounding buildings."

"Maybe we should weigh the cost of a little collateral damage," Ka'nak suggested.

"You'd be doing more than taking out property," San Roche warned, confirming what Jiya had feared earlier. "Sensors indicate there are a large number of hot spots, many small in size, in the nearest buildings. There's no way to take the Loranians out without hurting what I assume are local families."

"Which we're absolutely not going to do," Jiya stated before the Melowi warrior could argue.

"I agree." Reynolds shook his head. "We're not here to add to the misery, folks. Still, we need those crusty shitball Loranians captured. Any ideas?"

"I'm letting off another round of covering fire to keep their heads down," San Roche reported. "The gathered Orau to your left are insubstantial in number, only about eight crouched behind the next building over, then scattered numbers at all the buildings beyond there. If you can eliminate them, you've got a clear run to the end of the street and the Loranians on the other side."

"Can you keep the rest of them down and off our backs?" Reynolds asked.

"I believe so, yes," San Roche answered.

That was good enough for Jiya.

She bolted off, running in a crouch, weapon held before her as the shuttle ripped swirling, dusty craters in the street to cover her advance.

She rounded the corner with the crew at her heels to find the cowering Orau.

"Kill them quick!" one of the enemy shouted.

Those were the last words he ever spoke.

Jiya shot him in the chest, and he dropped without a sound. His companions returned fire wildly, energy bolts screaming in an attempt to avoid sharing his fate.

It did them no good.

Reynolds took a blast to the stomach, but he didn't so much as flinch before returning fire. His first shot blew the head off the soldier who'd blasted him, and Reynolds looked damn satisfied after doing it.

His second blast took out the guy behind him.

Geroux and Ka'nak finished off the rest, the Melowi grinning from the furor of combat.

He loved this stuff.

Before the bodies stopped twitching, San Roche came over the comm again. "You're clear the rest of the way down the street," he informed them.

The shuttle crept forward, angling for the best position to engage the largest possible number of enemy targets.

"We've got a small cluster of Orau soldiers building up at your backs now, so keep an eye on that," he told the crew. "If you're going to follow the Loranians, now would be a good time, before these guys find their courage again."

Jiya started off with a grunt of confirmation.

They charged down the street as San Roche provided cover. Though his efforts did little to cut down on the enemy soldiers, most of them smartly staying out of sight and the direct line of fire, the crew made good time since no one wanted to step out and challenge the fire superiority of the shuttle.

Jiya grinned at their good luck.

The grin left her face a moment later as a group of Orau emerged from behind another building, dozens of locals bound together in front of them, forming a living shield against the crew's weapons.

"Oh…hell no," Jiya growled, stumbling to a halt as the locals were paraded in front of them.

"Drop your weapons and surrender, or we kill the Krokans," one of the soldiers called.

"I guess they're considered Krokans too," Ka'nak remarked with a nod, clarifying what the crew had been wondering: what to call the locals. "Makes sense."

"What do you want to do?" Geroux asked.

There were too many people at risk to be cavalier about it and push on without a plan, no matter how badly she wanted to, but they couldn't let the Orau stall them.

"What we came here to do," Jiya answered, reaching behind her to pull something off her belt.

"We're not exactly prepared for a hostage situation," Ka'nak informed her.

Jiya nodded her agreement, but she wasn't going to sit around doing nothing.

"Then we improvise," she announced, cold determination in her voice.

With a flick of her wrist, she threw a device over the heads of the Orau.

CHAPTER THIRTEEN

"Sensors show the SD *Reynolds* is powering up a weapon I can't identify," the Loranian XO H'ron announced. "Power levels are off the charts, sir."

Jora'nal snarled, staring at the viewscreen and wishing his weapons had a tenth of the heat of his fury.

"A feint?" he asked.

"I don't think so, Master," H'ron replied, his face paling. "Energies continue to build."

"How long do we have?"

"A moment or two, little more," XO answered. "I can't be sure."

"Move all power into the shields as soon as they fire," Jora'nal ordered.

"Sir?" H'ron asked.

"You heard me," Jora'nal fired back, watching the *Reynolds* on the screen.

"I'm not sure we can take this…whatever it is, Master," H'ron argued.

"Have faith in Phraim-'Eh, XO," Jora'nal told him, grinning madly. "Our lord wants us to rid the galaxy of these scum," he explained. "He will not let us die so easily, H'ron."

It was clear XO was less certain than Jora'nal, but Jora'nal had faith. True faith.

Phraim-'Eh would see them through this.

"Don't waste the opportunity to do as much damage as possible to that Federation ship," Jora'nal commanded. "Keep hitting it until the last second."

"Master," H'ron muttered, then ordered the continued assault upon the superdreadnought.

There was little hope that the weapons of the *Pillar*, the Loranian cruiser, could effectively take out the Federation craft, but Jora'nal needed to test its capabilities to the fullest.

Along with the approaching Orau ships, Jora'nal could determine exactly what the superdreadnought in front of him was capable of. They needed only to survive whatever plans the SD *Reynolds* had for them.

"Their weapon has targeted us," H'ron called, desperation in his voice.

Jora'nal smiled. His god would not let them down.

He remained silent, standing at attention and staring at the SD *Reynolds*, waiting for the weapon to fire.

A great glowing ball of energy formed at the front of the superdreadnought and Jora'nal stiffened at seeing it.

There was *so* much power there.

He swallowed hard, but he wouldn't let these Federation scum intimidate him. The Voice of Phraim-'Eh had chosen him personally to lead this mission, and Jora'nal would not fail his master.

"Shields!" he screamed as the SD *Reynolds* released its fury upon them. "All power into the forward defenses."

It was as if the enemy had unleashed a miniature sun upon them.

That's when Jora'nal had his greatest moment of doubt.

His vision was wiped out by the enemy's fire as the blow struck dead on and the *Pillar* trembled as he'd never felt it before.

Jora'nal was knocked to the deck, the breath forced from his lungs as he struck the cold, unforgiving steel. He howled, blind, and scrambled to his seat by feel. The *Pillar* seemed ready to shake apart under the blow.

"Shields failing!" XO H'ron cried out as the ship was tossed about. "Twenty percent, ten…"

And then the last of the energy subsided and the wash of brilliance across the viewscreen faded, allowing Jora'nal to see at last.

He marveled at the power that had just engulfed them, its rage hitting the *Pillar* so quickly that the automated systems hadn't had time to react to the attack and darken the absolute brilliance that had nearly seared the eyes from Jora'nal's head.

"Shields are down, but the structural integrity of the hull remains high," H'ron reported with a quaver in his voice. XO clearly couldn't believe that they were still alive.

Jora'nal reserved the slightest bit of doubt.

How could anyone have survived that?

Yet they had, and Jora'nal stood on the bridge of his ship, alive and well.

"Hit them again!" he whooped, ordering a continued attack upon the Federation ship.

XO H'ron didn't question him.

The barrage started once more and the *SD Reynolds'* shields took the brunt of the attack this time, energy sparking off the gravitic defenses.

"Phraim-'Eh has graced us," Jora'nal called as they renewed their attack. "Can you not see it, H'ron?"

"I can, Master," XO replied without hesitation.

The ship rumbled as the SD *Reynolds* returned fire, having recovered from the energy use of their great weapon.

The forward armor began to buckle under the attack, and red lights and sirens filled the bridge. Jora'nal cursed and slammed a fist on the arm of his chair.

No matter how blessed he and his crew were, the captain knew damn well they could take little more without the energy shields. The enemy's weapons would tear the unprotected ship apart.

Though the *Pillar* had been specifically crafted by the followers of Phraim-'Eh to stand and challenge a ship like the superdreadnought, Jora'nal knew there was still only so much that could be accomplished.

That the *Pillar* had survived the unfathomable attack was a testament unto itself that the work Jora'nal was doing in the name of Phraim-'Eh was his god's will. Phraim-'Eh would have reveled in their blood had he not wanted Jora'nal to be the one to bring down the pathetic SD *Reynolds* and its crew.

"The fore hull is buckling, Master," H'ron called. "I've ordered the ship about, but we can't take much more of this without shields, sir. Hull integrity is dropping rapidly."

"I agree with your assessment," Jora'nal answered,

watching on the viewscreen as the Orau fighter-bombers arrived and began their assault upon the Federation super-dreadnought. "Activate the Gate drive and put some distance between us and the Federation ship, XO," Jora'nal ordered.

"And the Orau?" H'ron asked.

"It is up to Phraim-'Eh to save them as he did us," Jora'nal answered. "If our lord wants them to survive and conquer, then they will. It is not our concern."

"And our crew on the surface?" H'ron asked. "Do we simply leave them behind?"

"They knew the risks of the mission and have served their purpose, XO H'ron," Jora'nal replied. "We cannot wait for them to return."

"Master," H'ron answered, saying nothing more.

Jora'nal knew damn well he was abandoning the shuttle crew to their fate, but it didn't matter.

They were simply pawns in the overall scheme of things, and their deaths meant nothing to Jora'nal.

Nor did he believe they meant anything to Phraim-'Eh.

Jora'nal was the one who mattered to the god, and if there was a sacrifice to be made for the great deity, Jora'nal would gladly offer up the shuttle crew.

A Gate portal opened in front of the *Pillar* then, and the ship slipped through just as the *Pillar*'s scanners detected yet another building of energy from the *Reynolds*.

They were preparing their weapon once again, but they'd be too late.

The *Pillar* Gated away, the portal closing at its back.

"Now, Gate again here to confuse any attempt at following us," Jora'nal ordered.

His crew did as commanded, and the *Pillar* appeared at the fringes of the Krokus system once more, far enough out as to foil any attempts at tracking or scanning them.

Jora'nal slumped into his seat and let out a quiet sigh that none of his crew heard.

Despite his faith in Phraim-'Eh, the situation had been tenuous.

Another blow by that mighty weapon would have annihilated the *Pillar* and all aboard no matter what Phraim-'Eh's will might be.

Perhaps that was why the god had shown them they could survive a single blast—to ensure that Jora'nal did not underestimate the Federation scum. So that he could see their true potential and be ready.

And he would be.

The SD Reynolds *would fall at his hands,* he promised.

"Begin repairs and send a message to our benefactor," Jora'nal said. "If we're to do battle with that weapon we will need one of our own, and the means to withstand it for longer than a single moment."

"Yes, Master," XO H'ron called, issuing orders to the crew.

"Navigator V'ren," Jora'nal called, turning to face the crewmember. "Find us a dark hole to crawl into so we might lick our wounds and give thanks to the glory of our god."

The navigator barked an affirmative.

"We need to be renewed in both flesh and spirit before we go after the SD *Reynolds* again," Jora'nal went on. "And we will," he assured. "We will tear them from the stars at the behest of our god Phraim-'Eh."

Jora'nal stormed off the bridge, head held high.

Although he and his crew had been forced to flee the Federation's next attack, he had learned much in the confrontation.

The next battle would not be so decisive, nor would it go the way of the Federation.

This I swear, my lord!

CHAPTER FOURTEEN

The would-be assassins emerged from the crew's guest chambers, fury in their eyes.

Maddox had been correct. This wasn't a coup attempt. They had been there to kill Reynolds and the others.

The general's cheeks warmed at the threat and he made ready to attack, but the forces of President Jaer Pon arrived first.

Weapons fire erupted, filling the hallway, and Maddox ducked behind cover to keep from getting caught up in it. Best to let the presidential guard handle it, he imagined.

The armored acolytes, however, had other ideas.

They had come prepared for a real fight. They returned fire on the few guards, immediately putting them on the defensive.

The guards fell back, firing sporadically down the hall in a weak attempt to contain the acolytes.

It wasn't going to work, Maddox realized.

He heard the scuffle of feet close behind him.

"Trogol shit," he muttered under his breath and darted into the shadows, ducking to keep from being detected.

As soon as he settled, more guards stormed down the corridor from the direction Maddox had come. They charged around the corner and loosed a barrage of fire on the acolytes.

Maddox had to give it to the guards. Though they were clearly outclassed, they'd engaged and distracted the would-be assassins so more guards could flank them.

Whether it would be enough was yet to be seen.

It didn't take long for things to shake out.

The guards put up a fierce front, but they were simply unprepared for the ferocity of the acolytes, their training, and the weight of their numbers.

The crossfire between the two presidential guard squads whittled away at the acolytes, killing over half of them before they could retreat and take better cover, but the victory was short-lived.

The acolytes shifted from shooting the guards to shooting the ceiling above them.

Burst after burst of energy crashed into the ceiling, kicking up dust and debris, forcing the guards back.

Then the ceiling collapsed, dumping tons of stone and timber onto the heads of the guards hunkered down behind the wall.

There was a great rumble like an earthquake and screams followed, both going silent a moment later as the hall filled with wreckage and the guards died.

Maddox cursed under his breath as he watched the tide of battle shift.

He ducked farther into his shadowy hole and raised his weapon.

He couldn't be seen where he was because of his cloaking device, but he knew damn well the acolytes would be marching his way in mere moments now that the threat behind them had been silenced. Better to be safe, he felt.

The nearby presidential guards either didn't realize their time had come or were more loyal than smart. They held their ground as the acolytes turned their full focus on them and raced down the hallway, firing steadily as they moved.

To Maddox's surprise, the results ended more evenly than he'd expected.

When the last of the guards fell, only two of the acolytes were alive to claim victory.

A Pyrrhic victory, as the Reynolds AI had taught through his endless parade of military tactical and strategic training videos. Winning at the cost of all your people wasn't a win at all.

Both the acolytes were injured, although the wounds appeared minor.

They stumbled and cursed, kicking their way past the pile of dead guards and Maddox's location.

His first instinct was to take them out. It was combat, after all, and the victors were about to leave the field of battle.

It would be easy enough.

Neither of the acolytes had spotted him as they stumbled along, weary and distracted. They were just grateful to be alive.

Maddox could simply step out and kill both before they realized what had happened.

But what good would that do?

These acolytes had stormed the compound simply to attack and kill the crew, that much was clear.

Why?

Not knowing the answer to that made Maddox's stomach churn. *He had to know!*

Being a soldier, he'd been targeted for death more times than he could rightly remember. And although he could understand why an enemy would want him dead, the fact that these nameless, faceless assassins had come after the crew without any provocation pissed him off.

They had to have a reason.

This hadn't been some *wrong place, wrong time* scenario. No, the acolytes had come here purposely to attack and kill the crew.

Maddox wanted to know where they would go and what they would do now that their mission had failed.

He knew there was a chance they might return to the building where he'd seen them stage before the attack. If so, it would give him no new intel, but he needed to learn all he could. Reward outweighed the risk.

So, instead of killing them, he followed the pair as they limped out of the compound and back into the dark city streets.

They left the same way they'd entered, but it wasn't long before Maddox realized he'd made the right choice.

The pair veered off, heading a different direction than the one they'd come from. He followed them, still cloaked but careful nevertheless.

He couldn't afford for them to realize he was there. While he wasn't threatened by the two wounded acolytes, Maddox understood the chaos of combat.

As long as he remained invisible and undetected, he controlled the confrontation. He could step in and take out one of the acolytes before the other realized it had happened. Then he could capture the second of the pair easily enough and hope he could get what he wanted from him, but his military mind embraced the saying that hope was a lousy plan.

He had to avoid confrontation where there would always be uncertainty. They could get off a lucky shot, or he could be forced to kill them both. They could suicide if threatened with overwhelming force.

He didn't want that, so he followed at a discreet distance, watching where each foot fell so he could step in their tracks. He stayed away in case the stalwart suit's cloaking failed. It was already well past when he had expected to be revealed.

The general's decision and patience were rewarded a short time later when the two acolytes stumbled into a dark alley and slumped against the wall. While one caught his breath, the other dug in the trash at their feet.

He lifted a small device from the garbage and dusted it off. Maddox recognized it as a comm device.

"We have failed," the acolyte announced after triggering the device.

Only static answered him.

He waited a moment, casting furtive glances around him, before engaging the device once again.

"I repeat, we have failed," he said. "The off-worlders

were gone when we arrived. We've lost all but two of our number. Please advise."

Maddox hunkered down and waited as the two acolytes fidgeted in anticipation of an answer.

Just when the general believed it wouldn't be coming, a crackly voice resounded across the comm.

"Phraim-'Eh is disappointed in your failure," the voice announced with a sharpened edge. "The master is as well."

Phraim-'Eh? The master?

Maddox's thoughts whirled. He had no idea who either of those people might be or why they'd want the crew dead so badly.

He had to think these people were from Loran, given that the ship stalking them through space was. That couldn't be a coincidence, but how had they managed to reach out to the Krokans to pull off this attack?

And why?

There were far too many questions for Maddox to begin to answer on his own. Nothing made sense.

"Return to the manor," the voice went on, casting a chill in the air with its finality. "You must atone for your failure."

The acolyte holding the comm slumped against the wall beside his companion, the two sharing disappointed looks, shoulders hunched.

Maddox was surprised to see the acolyte lift the device to his mouth. "We are on our way," he announced, silencing the device and tossing it back into the trash.

The general couldn't imagine the consequence of failure as being anything less than death, yet these two marched away, clearly willing to accept their fate.

He was both impressed and annoyed by what that meant.

He'd expected to question to the two acolytes and pry what they knew out of them before they returned to their people. That the pair would willingly march back to their masters to face death meant they would not be easily broken, even by a person of Maddox's talents and experience.

These people were true disciples of a faith they whole-heartedly believed in.

Maddox had to act. The alley was dark and the pair hung their heads, unaware and vulnerable.

The general ran at them, body-blocking one into the wall. He punched the other in the gut, folding the shocked male in half. The first acolyte crumpled to the ground as Maddox turned off the cloak, grabbed the one standing, and pulled him upright until the two were face to face.

"Explain Phraim-'Eh," the general demanded, his knife hanging casually in his hand as the enforcer of his words. The acolyte lunged forward, and the general's training and reflexes took over. Maddox crouched and aimed the knife at his exposed midsection. The acolyte threw himself onto the blade and twisted. The knife pulled free when he fell to the ground.

"Zealots." The general growled his dismay before checking the surroundings to make sure he hadn't been seen. He stuffed the body behind the trash receptacle and lifted the other over his shoulder. "At least your *master* will think your courage failed you and you ran."

CHAPTER FIFTEEN

"Grenade!" Jiya shouted as she hurled the device and ducked.

"Wait!" Ka'nak called, one eye closed in contemplation. "I thought we didn't have any—"

Jiya grabbed his arm and hauled him behind cover.

Geroux and Reynolds did the same, the young tech covering her head as she curled up, near fetal.

Given what Jiya had done she thought that a bit excessive, but she couldn't blame her friend.

The Orau pushed their native shield forward and dove for cover as the metal device hurtled their direction. The captives stumbled and fell to the ground, entangled in their ropes.

"What about the—" Ka'nak started to ask but Jiya ignored him, jumping back to her feet and racing toward the scattering Orau.

"That wasn't really a grenade, was it?" Ka'nak asked.

Reynolds grinned and chased after Jiya, encouraging the others to follow. "Nope. It was a magazine."

Before the Orau had hit the ground and settled, Jiya was on them, gunning them down from point-blank range. She had no mercy for them, just as they'd shown no mercy for the poor innocent people they'd been using as flesh-shields.

The Orau, still expecting an explosion, were caught off guard by her ferocity.

She ran through, offing one after another as they lay prone, covering their heads, realizing far too late that the explosion had never occurred.

Reynolds and the crew joined her, shooting down the rest of the Orau as they scrambled to try to bring their weapons to bear.

It was too little, too late.

A moment later all the Orau were dead. Jiya went to help the captive Krokans, her hands raised to assure them she meant no harm.

She holstered her pistol, pulled a knife, and immediately started cutting the captives free. Wide eyes watched her as she did, unsure how to react.

Geroux joined her as Ka'nak and Reynolds stood guard.

"Still have eyes on the assholes?" Reynolds asked San Roche over the comm.

"Yes, sir," he answered right away, the shuttle hovering over the street and keeping the mass of Orau in hiding. "They're moving slowly and carefully. I have them in sight."

"Scan the streets for heat sources," Reynolds ordered. "They might have set or triggered traps along their route if they're going so slowly."

"Think they're luring us in?" Ka'nak asked.

"Entirely possible, but who knows?" Reynolds answered with a shrug. "We don't know enough about these people to know what they want. We can't assume they were prepared for us to be down here."

"We also can't presume they weren't," Jiya called after freeing the hostages.

"Exactly," Reynolds fired back. "Too many questions to know anything now."

"Do you know who any of the visitors were?" Geroux asked one of the captives.

The female shook her head, too afraid to say anything. Another stepped up in her stead.

"We've been hiding since the shuttle arrived," he said, gesturing toward the Loranian ship. "We know nothing of the Orau's visitors or their purpose here. We are but slaves."

"Not anymore," Jiya told them. "You and your people are free. Go tell the others," she said, nudging the former captives toward cover.

The Krokans hesitated, then ran without a glance back.

"You're promising them an awful lot. Are you certain they can provide for themselves?" Reynolds told her.

"I'm only offering them hope," she replied. "But if I have to burn down this planet and escort all these people back to Krokus 4 to ensure their safety, then that's what I'll do."

Reynolds raised his hands in surrender, grinning. "Fair enough, but they're sleeping in *your* quarters until we get there."

"These people shouldn't have to live like this," Jiya went on. "It's bad enough that the Orau have taken over their world, turning it into a trash fire while taking them hostage. But it's worse that Jaer Pon sent us to the planet without telling us they were here or that they had been enslaved.

"If I have to carry all of them home on my back and quarter them in the presidential suite, that's what's going to happen."

"Let's worry about the logistics of that once we find those shuttle-jumpers," Reynolds told her, gesturing over his shoulder.

"No traps or devices detected," San Roche reported then. "The group of Orau and the Loranian shuttle crew have settled into a building at the edge of the outpost. Unfortunately, there are a good number of Orau soldiers between them and you, and they're all under cover where I can't hit them without hurting innocents."

"Looks like we have to do this the old-fashioned way then," Reynolds muttered.

"And what's that?" Geroux asked.

"Run and gun," Ka'nak answered for Reynolds, smiling.

"That sounds...crappy," Geroux admitted.

"Not much choice unless you want to risk the shuttle landing and us flying it to our target.

"Not going to happen," Reynolds replied. "The second it sets down, it's vulnerable and every Orau in the area will target it. We won't even get a chance to say goodbye to San Roche before he goes up in a magnificent fireball."

"Then I guess that's out," Geroux replied, sighing.

"As long as he's up there, San Roche can cover us and negate the numbers advantage the Orau have on us,"

Reynolds explained. "Doesn't mean we're entirely safe, but it provides us the opportunity to go building to building and clear the enemy until we reach the one we need."

"During which time they are preparing to meet us," Geroux said, one eyebrow raised in concern.

"All the more reason for us to do this quickly," Ka'nak stated.

He started off without another word, darting out around the corner and racing toward the next building in line.

"Follow him," Reynolds ordered Jiya. "We'll circle around the other side."

Jiya nodded, gave her friend an enthusiastic smile, and shot off after the Melowi warrior.

Although she didn't want to leave Geroux behind, she knew the tech was as safe with Reynolds as anyone. In fact, she was probably safer since they were taking the less occupied route around the building.

Jiya didn't have time to worry about her friend for long, though.

A moment later, they engaged the enemy.

Five Orau stood there ready for them.

Ka'nak ran across the front of the alley, ducking and firing. He took one of the invaders by surprise and dropped him with a shot to the head. A second Orau returned fire and struck the Melowi. He grunted, but the blast didn't penetrate his armor.

That was when Jiya turned the corner.

She loosed a barrage of fire, killing the one who'd shot Ka'nak and wounding another.

Then they were all dead, quick as that after Reynolds and Geroux came up behind them.

"One down, about eight more buildings to clear," Ka'nak said with a laugh, starting off without waiting again.

"Stop!" Jiya ordered, bringing the warrior to a halt.

"We stay together," she ordered, growling at him. "We stand a better chance of winning if we do this as a team, not some random collection of assholes."

"Interesting visual aside, she's right," Reynolds stated. "We can't stand to lose anyone playing cowboy."

"I'm afraid I don't know that reference," Geroux complained.

"The maverick or the rebel," Reynolds clarified with a huff, remembering once again that none of his crew came from Earth. "Regardless, we stick together."

Ka'nak nodded to them and waited for the others to catch up.

Jiya offered him a grateful smile.

She'd been put in charge of these people and their lives. She was responsible for them, and she hadn't been taking that responsibility as seriously as she should have been.

Not any longer, she swore.

It was time for her to grow up, same as the rest of the crew.

"San Roche, follow us and engage any targets that present themselves, but keep an eye behind you. We don't want the Orau to sneak up on us."

She turned to Ka'nak. "You and I will continue up front like the last time, only more carefully, and Reynolds and Geroux can take the back."

Reynolds nodded his agreement with her decision, and he even waited for her to signal their departure before they set out.

Jiya swallowed hard as she and the Melowi warrior made their way along the building toward the next waiting enemy.

She was glad Reynolds had seen fit to let her take charge, and she promised herself she'd earn it by doing it right. None of her crew would die on this mission.

As they approached the corner, Jiya triggered her comm. "Any Krokans in the building to my right?" she asked.

"Negative," San Roche came back a second later.

Jiya grinned and raised her weapon, firing bolt after bolt through the wall in the direction of the Orau hiding behind it. Screams rang out, and Jiya motioned Ka'nak forward.

The warrior went with a smile on his lips.

He stepped around the corner to find the Orau retreating and ducking to avoid being shot by the unexpected gunfire ripping through the building. Ka'nak added his weapon's voice to the chaos, shooting down the handful of Orau before Geroux and Reynolds cleared the far corner.

The pair arrived to find everyone dead.

"Seven more," Ka'nak counted, but this time he waited for the others before he ran off.

Shuttle fire continued to blast the streets around them as San Roche covered their approach.

It was still a long way to their target, the shuttle occupants hiding in the last building on the street, and there was plenty of time for things to go wrong.

Jiya decided that wasn't going to happen.

They'd clean up the scum that were the Orau and the crew from the Loranian shuttle.

At the last building before engaging the Loranian crew, Jiya caught shrapnel to the neck that charred her skin and made it hard for her to turn her head all the way to the right, and Ka'nak was shot in the arm.

San Roche flew the shuttle closer and threatened to unload on the Orau who had turned the tide in the enemy's favor, and the bluff worked perfectly.

As soon as the shuttle roared above, the last of the Orau's discipline gave way and the ranks broke. No longer covering each other, they became most intent upon fleeing; the soldiers threw their weapons down and ran. Those who fought died quickly without the cover fire of their fellows.

The Loranian hideout was easily twice the size as any of the other buildings at the outpost. It was also better defended, and made of stone and steel rather than the wood of the other huts and buildings.

There were a number of murder holes for windows, and although Jiya could not see anyone peeking out of them, she could feel their presence as she hunkered behind cover.

"Head-on looks like it's out," Ka'nak advised, putting words to what they were all thinking. "They've cleared a killing field in front of this place." He gestured to the open terrain between the building they lurked behind and the one they needed to get to.

"Yeah, I think I've been shot enough for one day," Jiya agreed, rubbing her neck.

"Our targets are still in the building, right, San Roche?" Reynolds asked over the comm.

"Affirmative, sir," the shuttle pilot replied. "There are twenty Orau, five passengers from the shuttle, and unfortunately, about twenty local Krokans, too."

"Gralflie tits," Jiya growled. "These guys are starting to piss me off."

"Just *starting*? What's the plan?" Geroux asked, staring at the building.

"We use the shuttle to distract them," Jiya suggested when she heard it approaching. "We let San Roche pressure them and—"

A thought clicked in her head, and her eyes shot wide.

"Oh…shit!"

"What is it?" Geroux's alarm raised her voice an octave.

The comm crackled before Jiya could get explain.

"The Loranian shuttle is coming straight at me," San Roche shouted.

"Bring up the trigger," Jiya ordered, and Geroux scrambled at her wrist to comply, fingers flying across the datapad.

As soon as the explosive detonator was up, Ka'nak pushed past Reynolds and tapped the controls.

The Loranian shuttle exploded mid-flight before it reached San Roche, going down in a ball of flame in the middle of the street. There was a tremendous crash and fire and sparks danced about, threatening to engulf the outpost.

"What?" he asked as everyone stared at him. "You said I could push the button."

"Damn it!" Jiya watched the flames spread. "We aren't trying to burn the place down. We need to put that fire out."

"I think we might have more important things to worry about," Geroux mentioned, gesturing toward the sky.

Beyond the city a legion of missiles streaked into the sky, leaving behind trails of smoke and fire as they headed for space.

"They're attacking the *Reynolds*?" Jiya asked, her heart pounding at seeing the missiles rise.

Reynolds shook his head. "I don't think so," he answered. "Given the angle, it's more likely they're bombarding Krokus 4 again."

"They're hoping we'll pull back," Ka'nak stated.

"That's not going to happen," Reynolds replied. He reached out to Captain Asya through Comm. "Can we shut these missiles down, Captain?"

"Little busy right now," she answered, and the crew could hear the sounds of battle in the background. "Mopping up the Orau ships at the moment, but we'll take out as many of the missiles as we can while we're here. Then we'll start in on the sites, but it isn't going to happen right away if you want us to keep the ship in one piece. Mostly."

"Do your best," Reynolds growled, cutting the link. "Looks like it's on us, people."

The Loranian shuttle crew and the last of the Orau fled, the two groups racing in different directions.

"I've had enough of these sandy assholes," Reynolds shouted, realizing the Orau had been delaying them long enough to launch their barrage and to send the automated shuttle after them as a distraction.

"Go after those missiles," Reynolds ordered San Roche. "Sit in high orbit and kill as many as you can. Buy my ship time to clear the Orau."

"What do you want us to do?" Ka'nak asked.

"A couple of these damn launch sites are smack dab in the center of this outpost," he replied. "That means there are civilians. We need to eliminate those to minimize casualties. Asya can't hit these sites without causing significant collateral damage."

Jiya nodded, understanding the situation. "Ka'nak, you and Geroux hit that one over there." She pointed toward the nearest of the contrails leading back to the site. "Reynolds and I will—"

Reynolds shook his head. "You're on your own, Jiya," he countered. "We need to catch the Loranian shuttle crew before they slip away. That's on me," he stated, racing off before anyone could argue.

"Then that's how it'll be," she said, gesturing for Ka'nak and Geroux to take off. "I'll get the other site. Stay in contact on comm so we can rendezvous once we're done."

Ka'nak and Geroux dashed away, picking up speed on their way toward the center of the settlement. Jiya hesitated for just a moment, watching as Reynolds disappeared around a corner as he chased the Loranian shuttle crew.

What had been a simple plan to capture the aliens and nuke the missile sites had turned into a clusterfuck of titanic proportions.

With San Roche no longer providing air support, the crew were on their own. She needed to disable the launch sites, rendezvous with her crew, free the planet from Orau rule, and return to Krokus 4.

She decided that she'd better get started.

Jiya ran off before the cowering Orau figured out her top cover was gone.

She had a missile site to take out.

That suited her mood perfectly.

CHAPTER SIXTEEN

"We've lost them!" XO called. "The Loranian cruiser has Gated."

Asya snarled. "Any way to track those fuckers?" she asked.

"Not while we've got these Orau shitstains strafing us," Tactical answered. "While those Loranian twits didn't collapse our shields, they sure as hell kicked them in nicely. We're actually taking damage from these fighter-bombers."

"Then draw power from the engines if you need to and reinforce our shields," Asya ordered. "If we can't chase the cruiser, we need to swat these flies before someone gets hurt."

"I still can't believe they survived that," Ensign Ria said, eyes wide as she worked her console.

"Neither can I," Tactical admitted, for once stating something without sarcasm. "They took the ESD and shrugged it off."

"Not exactly," Asya clarified. "We took out their shields

and did some damage after the fact, so it wasn't a complete waste of effort."

"No, you don't understand. The ESD is effective against Kurtherian technology. It has been used to destroy Yollin superdreadnoughts. There is no defense against it. Something must have gone wrong with the weapon. I wonder if Gorad planted a virus when he was fucking around in my guts?" XO snarled.

"Running a diagnostic on the system now," Tactical reported.

"We knew they were different from the start since they tracked us through our Gate," Asya replied, "but we're going to have to worry about that later. Scanners are picking up a sortie of missiles being launched from the planet's surface."

"That's not it," Tactical bemoaned. I've found the code that was latched onto the ESD power system. The ESD fired at ten percent effectiveness. The system is down until I can strip the bullshit from the control programming. I'll do that as soon as we put these Orau fucks in their place."

Comm interrupted. "Got Reynolds on the line."

"On speaker," Asya replied.

"Can we shut these missiles down, Captain?" Reynolds asked.

"Little busy right now," she answered, and the crew could hear the sounds of battle in the background. "Mopping up the Orau ships at the moment, but we'll take out as many of the missiles as we can while we're here. Then we'll start in on the sites, but it isn't going to happen right away if you want us to keep the ship in one piece. Mostly."

"Do your best," Reynolds growled, and the comm went silent.

"That went well," Tactical quipped. Asya gave the empty tactical seat the finger, a gesture she'd picked up from watching human videos. She liked using it as an all-inclusive, word-saving retort.

"Like he said, we'll do what we can." Asya shrugged. "Tactical, split your efforts between the missiles that reach space and the Orau," she ordered, spying the shuttle inserting itself between the missiles and open space.

"There are more Orau fighter-bombers incoming," Ria announced. "They're rising from the far side of the planet."

"Can a superdreadnought fight off blood-sucking bugs?" Asya growled. "It didn't work out well for that death star, but we're not one of those, are we ladies and gentlemen?"

No one replied.

As Asya contemplated the state of affairs, Tactical turned the superdreadnought into a fantastic display of energy-fueled weapons. The closest Orau fighter-bombers vanished in the first few milliseconds, then the next concentric ring.

Missiles launched through the engagement zones, racing after the Orau missiles that had gotten past San Roche. Tactical whooped and catcalled as he spun his death dance.

Even after that awesome display, there are still too damn many to count, Asya thought. And they kept coming.

"These guys are like fucking hyenas," Tactical muttered.

"What are those?" Ria asked.

"Smaller predators who run in packs to take down larger foes," XO explained.

"They're going to need more than they have," Asya declared, pumping her fist as Tactical took out another wave of Orau ships.

"Fuck, yeah, they are," Tactical agreed. The superdreadnought's weapons slowed. *Bolero* started to play over the bridge's speakers. Asya raised her hand to stop it, but the building tempo caught her attention. Tactical started cycling through the *Reynolds'* weapons systems in time to the music.

Ensign Ria picked up on the pace and maneuvered to bring the Orau ships into the most lethal engagement zones.

"Fuck, *yeah!*" Tactical cheered. Asya leaned back and watched. She'd never seen anything like it. The firepower. The dance of death. The enemy that refused to give up. Missiles. A crew stranded on the planet.

"Rest gently, enemy mine," she cooed softly at the Orau ships. "You'll not have to worry about anything ever again. And then we'll be on our way." She smiled darkly as the Orau ships died before the onslaught unleashed by her assmouthed tactical officer.

The one good thing about an AI was that no matter how much Tactical gloated or talked shit, he never stopped fighting.

"Got one of the missiles," Tactical called, but there was no excitement in his voice. "There are too many of them, though. San Roche is doing well, taking them out, but his weapons are limited and these damn things are smart, staying at extreme range from us."

"Then we're going to have to hope that Krokus 4's shield can defend against whatever gets past us," Asya replied, but then a thought hit her. "Helm, send a couple of the Pods out and chase those things down before they get too far. Maybe we can cut down on how many make it all the way to Krokus 4."

"On it," Helm replied. Asya was glad the AI personality hadn't completely shut down when Ria had taken over his post.

He'd assumed a passive stance, which spoke more to the condition of Reynolds' brain than Helm's functionality, fortunately.

Asya watched as three of the SD *Reynolds'* Pods launched from the hangar bay and raced after the missiles that had gotten by.

"Keep those bomber fucks away from the Pods," Asya ordered Tactical.

"As if I don't have enough to do?" Tactical shot back. Ria reoriented the ship to keep it between the bombers and the Pods.

"I'm thinking you need more," Asya told him.

She wasn't sure how limited the AI personalities were while separated from the main consciousness that was Reynolds. She couldn't risk overwhelming any of them.

So, rather than have Tactical fire on the missile sites, she took the job on. She fiddled with the console, transferring partial fire controls to her post so he didn't have to bother with it. She tagged the crew's location, aimed, calculated trajectories, adjusted for conditions, and started lobbing missiles at the planet below.

Tactical took out another of the Orau then, leaving only

two flitting near the *Reynolds*. Annoyed by their nagging presence, she redirected a couple of her missiles at one of the Orau, grinning as they struck it broadside and sent the ship tumbling.

Tactical annihilated it seconds later.

"Great shot!" Asya called. "Now wipe that last piece of shit off our heel and focus on those damn missiles."

"That was like a pat on the back and a kick in the ass at the same time," Tactical muttered. "I think I liked it."

"Of course you did," Asya shot back, but she couldn't stop smiling. She launched another missile at a launch site on Krokus 1. And then another.

Tactical focused on the last fighter-bomber, trailing it as the ship tried to circle over the top of the superdreadnought to avoid the big guns. It thereby brought itself into the range of the array of canons designed to protect the ship against a maneuver exactly like that one, however.

The ship exploded, debris and vented atmosphere swirling in a murky cloud where the ship had been a moment before.

Tactical immediately went back to targeting the missiles shrieking up from the planet.

Asya noted that a second wave had joined the first, then a third was launched.

She growled. "Pretty persistent bunch down there."

"Those guys are getting ready to pound us worse than a sailor on shore leave," Tactical remarked.

"That disturbing image aside, kill the missiles in flight. I'll keep targeting the launch sites," Asya ordered.

Takal came over the comm right then. "I've been monitoring the battle, Captain," he told her, "and I might have an idea."

"Is it a good one?" Tactical asked.

"I wouldn't have bothered you if it weren't," the old inventor fired back.

"Humility is dead on this ship," XO announced.

"What have you got in mind?" Asya asked.

"It's a simple task where I reverse the polarity on these pucks that Reynolds pointed out to me yesterday and then invert the—"

"In small words, please," Asya told him, her head swimming with what he was trying to get at.

"My apologies. Of course. These pucks are apparently used for blasting through doorways and walls and whatever else needs to be blasted through. They have a magnetic clasp that holds them in place, and while they would hardly be sufficient to blow through the hull of an armored ship on their own, they might very well be—"

"You're getting to the point soon, right?" Tactical asked. "*Any* point. The point?"

"I am indeed," Takal assured. "I can make the pucks leak their energy instead of explode."

"Which means shit-all to me, Takal," Asya told the inventor. "Give me the so-what right fucking now!"

"We can launch them at the Orau weapons and trigger them."

"Like lighting off sparklers on the sides of the missiles!" XO shouted. "I love it."

"Forgive me my ignorance, XO, but how the hell is that going to help us? These missiles aren't heat-seeking."

"No, not precisely, but they do have very simple

targeting mechanisms," Takal explained. "They're on a precise course, which has very little room for error or distraction. The magnetic field of the pucks, along with the distribution of its internal energies, will confuse the systems enough to throw them off course."

"Why don't we just use the pucks to kill the ships and the missiles?" Asya asked.

"We don't have enough for both. We're only just now rebuilding the puck inventory. We need more raw materials, but we don't make many friends out here who are willing to sell them to us," Takal ended with a hearty harrumph.

"And since the Orau believe they know exactly what lanes the missiles are taking, we might just take out a number of the fighter-bombers with their own fucking artillery," XO finished.

"But doesn't that leave us at risk, too?" Ria asked.

Asya could practically hear Takal shrug on the other end of the comm.

"Well, it does, of course, but we are both prepared for the eventuality and better equipped to deal with the detonation of these missiles than either the Orau ships or the Krokus 4 homeworld, are we not?" Takal asked.

"I suspect I'll regret this order, but do what you need to make this work, Takal," Asya commanded. "Round up whoever you need to help you."

"It's a simple task," he replied, disconnecting the comm.

"Says the guy opening us up to more damage," Tactical laughed. "Maybe he doesn't realize the lab is between us and the missiles at this angle."

"We just need to direct more energy to the shields

downward," Asya said. "It's not like we don't know where the missiles are coming from."

"And then we need to keep the Orau from getting on top of us and exploiting the opening," XO went on. "Can you do that, Tactical?"

"Oooh, a psychological challenge to question my ego and get me to agree to this stupidity at the same time," Tactical shot back. "You're about as subtle as a hammer to the face, XO."

"So you'll do it?" XO asked.

"Of course I will," Tactical replied. "I'm a sucker for a lost cause."

"Then we're agreed? Stupid plan for the win?" Asya asked.

"Looks that way," XO agreed, chuckling.

"Reynolds is going to kill us, yeah?" Asya moaned.

"As long as we don't blow the ship up doing it he won't care," Tactical stated. "Not right away, at least. I'm just glad I can't be confined to my quarters and made to eat quarter rations."

Asya sighed. If that was what it took, so be it.

"Just do it, and we can pin the blame on me if shit goes south."

"There's always the hope that you'll die a horrible death in flaming wreckage before Reynolds gets back," Tactical told her.

"And on that positive note, let's get to work, people," Asya ordered.

She watched the scanners as scores of missiles streaked upward, desperate to reach Krokus 4 and lay waste to the already fragile shield keeping the citizens from the ravages of the ocean surrounding them.

Hell, this is what I signed up for, isn't it?

Not exactly, but you have to look at the bright side, right?

Right?

Dammit! Am I talking to myself as if there's more than one of me? Fucking Reynolds!

CHAPTER SEVENTEEN

Jiya stalked through the town, wishing she had one of the cloaking devices integrated into her suit.

She'd have to get Takal to remedy that shortcoming once they got back. The thing was quite useful, judging by what she'd seen Maddox pull off earlier. She could have put the device to good use.

Instead, she'd been made to creep carefully through the darkened alleys, taking out Orau when she could and avoiding them when she couldn't.

It made the trip much longer than she'd anticipated.

Once she arrived, she realized she could have taken even more time, seeing how she wasn't remotely prepared for what lay ahead of her.

Damn it, she thought, eyes wide as she spied the launch site.

Nestled between a cluster of close buildings, the site was manned by six Orau, but there were dozens of local Krokans strung up by their wrists around the site, making it so Jiya couldn't get an easy shot off. The enemy had built a low stone wall around themselves in addition to keeping hostages along the outside.

The Krokans stood on their tiptoes, uncomfortable as they were made to defend the Orau from attack. Blood dripped from the arms of several of the captives, and Jiya's stomach churned at seeing it run in red rivulets down their arms and across their chests.

She growled low in her throat, wishing she could simply direct the *Reynolds* to light up the site, but that would kill everyone there.

She couldn't do that.

Jiya inched forward to take a better look at the Orau as they readied another missile for launch. They worked in tandem, one of them pacing the area in a tight circle and keeping watch while the others prepared the weapon.

Jiya tried to figure what angle would be best to approach the site when she spotted Orau on each of the nearby roofs overlooking the launch location. They peeked out every now and again, surveying the area.

She growled again, realizing they'd covered the most obvious approaches, and from her position, she couldn't tell if there was more than a single soldier on all the roofs. She took a moment to examine the sides of the buildings facing the site and noticed that all of them were solid walls, with no windows or doors leading her closer to the Orau preparing the weapons or their hostages.

Not that it mattered.

As she contemplated her next move, she spotted movement inside the nearest building and cursed under her breath, nearly biting her tongue in the process.

The Orau had set up guards inside the surrounding buildings as well as on top of it, effectively cutting off every approach.

Work smarter, not harder.

She chuckled nervously as her brain parsed an idea, but the more she thought about it, the more her mind seized on it.

Am I really that crazy or desperate? she wondered.

To her regret, she had to admit that she was just enough of both to pull her plan off.

If it didn't work, she wouldn't have to worry about Reynolds being pissed at her since she'd be dead.

She waited until the rooftop guards had made their rounds, then sneaked around the building and made her way toward the one nearest the others.

"What do I have to lose?" she whispered to herself, laughing.

"Just my life" was the answer she refused to supply, but she knew she had to do something.

She was the only chance the hostages had of making it home alive tonight. There was no way she wouldn't do her best to make that happen, even if it put her at risk.

"Fuck it."

———

Geroux and Ka'nak made their way through town toward the site they'd been assigned to eliminate.

Several missiles launched from it while they traveled, and each one was a nail driven into Geroux's spine.

She hated the idea that each of those missiles represented lives being lost somewhere on Krokus 4. Her fists clenched the whole time, she'd wanted to rush to the site and start kicking ass, but Ka'nak held her back.

It was a good thing he had.

As they drew closer to the site, Geroux realized the Melowi had been right. She had thought that the sites, given how numerous they were, wouldn't be heavily guarded.

She was wrong.

She counted twenty Orau soldiers surrounding the site, the location squeezed between a number of closely arranged buildings. A handful of soldiers worked on loading one of the nearby missiles while the remainder patrolled the area, staying close to each other with interlocking fields of fire.

"That's a lot of soldiers," Geroux muttered as they found a place to hunker down and make a plan.

Ka'nak grunted his agreement, his head on a swivel as he tried to find the best way to accomplish their mission of destroying the site.

He seemed to come to a decision a moment later, glancing over his shoulder at Geroux.

"How's your confidence today?" he asked.

She offered a weak smile. "If you're asking how I feel about taking on a squadron of armed soldiers, I have to admit my confidence is not all that high."

The Melowi laughed low in his throat. "You don't need to take them all on—" he started.

"That's good, then."

"You need only to hold them off and distract them for a few moments," Ka'nak finished.

Geroux sighed. "So I don't have to fight them all, I just have to engage them and wait for something else to happen while letting them shoot at me?" she asked.

"Exactly," Ka'nak replied.

"I have to admit, I'm not really liking this plan," she told him.

"Well, it's all we've got," he shot back, starting down the alley toward the street they'd just come from. "Be ready for my signal."

What's your signal, and what are you going to do? she asked over the comm as the warrior disappeared around the corner.

I'll tell you to engage them, of course, he replied a moment later.

"Brilliant," she moaned, wondering what the hell she'd gotten herself into.

I wonder if it's too late to find a desk job somewhere?

Reynolds followed the Loranian shuttle crew, bound and determined to capture at least one of them to see what they were there for and why the ship had been following them.

He needed that answer. His search for Kurtherians was the only reason he was in the Chain Galaxy, and the Loranians had information he needed. His road to mission accomplishment went through them.

Separated from their Orau companions, the shuttle crew circled back on the outpost, pushing toward the more crowded area they'd already been through. With no shuttle to return to since Ka'nak had blown it up,

Reynolds could not fathom what the shuttle crew was up to.

He followed, gaining ground and getting closer to the crew, observing them all the while. He was curious as to where they were leading him, only to realize he'd probably made a mistake not attacking them sooner.

The crew darted off unexpectedly after having moved at a measured pace for the first while, and Reynolds saw them slip inside a small building in the middle of the outpost.

Unlike the other buildings in the area, this one had numerous windows along its sides.

Reynolds dashed to the building and pressed his back against the wall, peeking inside as he heard voices rise up in terror.

They were the voices of children.

Reynolds cursed as he spotted the shuttle crew gathering a small group of Krokan children and their apparent teacher, pulling them into a tight knot. They held weapons to the heads of the kids and moved slowly toward the exit on the other side of the building. They spotted Reynolds through the window and kept their hostages between him and them.

That was Reynolds' first real look at the scumbags who had flown down from the Loranian cruiser.

He was surprised to note that only two were Loranian. The other three were races he was unfamiliar with.

The one who appeared to be in charge looked as if his skin were a melted candle. Layers of reddened flesh ran across his features, the skin glistening at his furious expression.

His eyes were gleaming balls of yellow like a pair of shining suns. They radiated hatred as he watched Reynolds stalk them outside.

Reynolds could relate.

"Your time has come," Reynolds warned loud enough for the crew to hear him through the windows.

A second alien sneered at the AI. He might as well have been a ghost, given how pale he was. As white as the wall at his back, the alien abductor pressed his weapon against the head of a little crying female as he and his companions filed out of the building.

Reynolds followed, the sounds of the children crying lighting a fury inside him he couldn't remember having ever felt. He moved toward the crew, stepping out from behind the cover of the building as the pack of kidnappers and hostages backed into the street.

"You have signed your own death warrants," Reynolds declared.

"Did Metalhead say something?" the ghost taunted. Reynolds understood the language, so the species was in someone's database. He'd dig them out when he had time.

"Let the kids go," Reynolds warned. "Last chance."

"Not going to happen," Melted Face replied, grinding his gun barrel into the head of a little male, making the child scream.

That was the last straw as far as Reynolds was concerned.

He spun and raced behind the school building, out of sight of the shuttle crew and their hostages. The children were in danger as long as he was there, but the crew of the Loranian cruiser had left him no option.

He needed to act, and he needed to act *now*.

Jiya climbed up the outside of the building and pulled herself over the top to find the roof unoccupied. She took a deep breath, let the air fill her lungs, then ran with everything she had toward the ledge of the building opposite the one that flanked the missile site.

Even though she stayed low, she knew it was only a matter of time until the guard on the roof across the way spotted her. Every second counted, so she pushed harder and caught sight of the Orau's wide eyes as he saw her charging and realized at the last moment what she intended.

She hit the ledge and leapt, flying over the space between the buildings.

The guard raised his weapon as she hurtled through the air, but Jiya was prepared.

She tapped her trigger, her gun already out and aimed, and shot him center mass as she'd been taught. Hit the biggest target and follow up with the kill shot if the enemy wasn't already dead.

He staggered back, smoke wafting from his armor. He tried to regain his balance, but Jiya shot him again.

The guard collapsed, his weapon slipping free of his dead hand and skittering across the roof.

Jiya struck the roof a moment later, channeling her momentum into a forward roll that carried her to the middle before the guards on the other buildings started shooting at her.

The bursts of energy flew harmlessly over her head as she grinned, unable to contain her excitement.

The leap had been nearly nine meters, and she hadn't been sure she could make it when she first decided on her plan. Fortunately, the suit's augmented frame had done as she'd hoped and carried her across the void.

Her leap landed her directly above the site, and despite the weapons fire headed her way, she felt certain she still held some small window of surprise over the Orau warriors stationed below.

A missile rose in a cloud of smoke, engines roaring, drowning out the chaos happening above.

Jiya had timed it perfectly.

As the rocket flew toward space, she rolled to the western edge of the building and rose to a knee, sending burst after burst of energy at the guard across the way.

He went down under the barrage, and Jiya focused on the next guard. She crept along the wall, staying below the cover of the ledge, and positioned herself where she felt she'd get the best shots.

She waited for a moment, forcing herself to sit there longer than she wanted to before finally popping up and strafing the roof across from her.

The guard returned fire as soon as he saw her, but her armor was better, even if her aim wasn't.

A blast slammed into her arm and staggered her. She bit back a pained scream as the new wound sent flares of agony racing up her shoulder and into her neck to join the wound that was already there.

It won't be that easy, she promised.

She dug deep and fired once more, hitting the guard as he tried to shoot her again.

Feral satisfaction washed through her as the guard stumbled and fell back on the roof, no longer moving.

One more, she thought, and her feet were already running before she could argue.

She didn't give the last guy a chance to zero in on her.

With quick taps of her trigger, she fired dozens of shots across the space between the roofs and peppered her opponent with blasts of energy.

He went down in a hail of gunfire before he'd managed a single return shot.

Jiya stumbled to the ledge, catching her breath as she peeked over, looking down at the assembled Orau readying another missile for the launcher. The hostages trembled, terror etched on their features, and Jiya felt the knots in her stomach growing hard as rocks.

Now all I have to do is to eliminate five Orau before they kill any of the hostages, she thought, staring hard at the people below.

Easy, right?

"Now, Geroux," Ka'nak shouted over the comm.

Geroux swallowed her doubts and eased around the corner of the building. She aimed and squeezed the trigger.

She knew if she hesitated for even a second, gave in to the nagging worry that threatened to consume her, she would sit there and do nothing and the Orau would win.

She couldn't have that.

Instead, she did as Ka'nak wanted her to and engaged the Orau before they realized she was there.

One of the Orau was shot in the back, and he staggered forward screaming. A second Orau went down, then a third as she fired without mercy, raining hell on the unsuspecting soldiers.

The element of surprise lasted little more than a heartbeat.

They spun and dove for what little cover they could find before returning fire. Geroux ducked behind the wall as dozens of energy blasts ripped into it. Shards of wood and dust peppered her as she crouched, waiting for a lull in the onslaught and the opportunity to fire back.

That came seconds later.

She heard screams from the mass of Orau soldiers and the attack on her position ceased as quickly as it had begun.

Geroux cautiously peered around the corner to see Ka'nak wreaking havoc in the midst of the Orau.

He shouted his battle cry as he attacked. Gun in his left hand, he darted through their confused ranks, shooting them up close and personal. Those he couldn't shoot, he attacked with his other hand and knees and feet.

He spun through the enemy, bloody fists slamming like pistons, crashing into faces and breaking bones.

The Melowi warrior gave the Orau no room to escape.

Like a storm of violence, he cut a swath through the enemy.

Within seconds he had wiped out half of the Orau, leaving the others scrambling.

The Orau had just started to organize when Geroux hit them from behind.

Careful not to hit the whirlwind that was Ka'nak, she targeted those on the fringe of the group, pelting them with weapons fire. Caught between the fury that was the Melowi and Geroux's discharge they died quickly, barely aware of what had killed them.

Geroux dropped to her knees as Ka'nak went to work on the missile launcher, disabling it with brutally efficient blows. When it gave way, she sighed in relief, a grin stretching her cheeks. Ka'nak roared his fierce cry of victory.

Maybe she wouldn't need the desk job after all.

Jiya steeled her nerves and jumped before she could talk herself out of it.

Fortunately, gravity was on her side this time.

That was what happened when you jumped off a building.

She gritted her teeth as she soared through the air—well, soared might be too graceful a word.

It was more like she fell like an awkward stone, but she hadn't held high hopes for the maneuver to begin with.

As she careened toward the cluster of Orau soldiers below, she targeted the one farthest from the group. He didn't even notice her as she blew his head off.

The others, however, saw her, and their weapons started to come up toward her hurtling figure. She crashed into their ranks, bowling them over after colliding with a solid *thunk*.

She bit back a grunt as pain flared, her spine crunching into the launcher, limbs flailing.

As much as the impact hurt, she couldn't help but savor the joy as the Orau crawled around her trying to regain their senses.

She didn't let them. With the Orau guards eliminated, Jiya started cutting the hostages down, freeing them from the chain of limbs that tied them together in a circle around the site.

She flopped to the ground as the last of the Krokans was released, grunting in pain from the injuries she'd sustained during the attack. They gathered around her, rubbing their wrists and muttering thanks with wide and grateful eyes.

Too tired and sore to join in their growing jubilation, she gestured toward the missile launcher with her chin.

"You guys want to break something for me?"

The Krokans leapt to the task with relish, using the dropped Orau weapons as Jiya looked on, laughing all the while.

CHAPTER EIGHTEEN

Reynolds circled the school and darted across the street in an attempt to flank the Loranian crew and their child hostages.

As badly as he wanted to teach the bastards a lesson in brutality, he knew better than to put the kids at risk.

He pressed his android body to its fullest as he circled around his enemy, knowing Takal would need to focus his full attention on a replacement. There was no way it would hold up much longer, given how much damage had been done to it and how much he demanded of it.

Inherent in all AI programs that Bethany Anne sanctioned was the requirement to protect children. Reynolds knew he couldn't risk their lives. He'd been programmed that way. As long as the children were in danger, Reynolds would do whatever it took to rescue them safely, even if it meant sacrificing his mobility.

I can always plug back into the Jonny-Taxi body.

With that disgusting thought in his head, he zigzagged

back around the shuttle crew, staying out of sight while they cast glances around to find him. Their anxiety rose with each step where they didn't know his location.

Reynolds swore he would kill all the shuttle crew to save the children, even if it meant not capturing one to interrogate.

"Don't think you can stop us, heathen," the melted-face male taunted. "These kids'll be dead before you can do so much as—"

Reynolds killed him first.

He hit him so hard and fast that the alien was dead before the final word left his mouth.

Reynolds unleashed his fury.

With perfect precision, Reynolds hurled the corpse down the line of the Loranian crew. It slammed into the others in rapid, bone-jarring succession.

The shuttle crew grunted and groaned as their companion bounced off them, plowing them aside. The last in line managed to squeeze off a shot, but he'd been knocked to his knees and the shot had gone into the air.

The kids screamed and scattered, and only four enemy and Reynolds remained. He had to maintain the initiative to finish this before the crew reacted.

Reynolds stomped the face of the nearest crew member. The AI ignored the brittle snap of bones and kicked the next in line in the ribs, following that with a gunshot to the head.

The last two scrambled to get back to their feet, raising their weapons and firing, but Reynolds shrugged off the impacts. He grabbed the wrist of the first crewmember and bent it back as he fired a second time.

His face looked worse after it absorbed a close-range blast from his own pistol.

Reynolds flung his body aside and went to grab the last of the living Loranian crew, but he was too slow.

The crewmember squeezed off a shot...

But it wasn't at Reynolds.

Kids screamed as their teacher was struck in the back while shielding target: a little female who lay trapped in her teacher's arms as she collapsed.

With a growl that sounded more like a volcano erupting, Reynolds stepped in front of the next shot, taking it full in the chest.

The blast warped the metal there and sensors went off, warning him of internal damage, but the end was in sight.

He crushed the weapon in the male's hand, along with his fingers.

The alien shrieked, and Reynolds drove his fist into his face so hard that his head snapped backward, his jaw broken and crushed by Reynolds' armored hand.

The body dropped to the ground.

Reynolds kicked him in the face out of spite and spun, running over to the fallen teacher's side.

He breathed a sigh of relief to find her alive.

"I...I..." She tried to speak, but Reynolds hushed her.

He rolled her over, freeing the young female and making sure she was okay. He let out another sigh when he realized she was okay.

All of them were.

The children huddled around him, terrified but alive and unharmed.

He returned to the Loranian, hauling him roughly to his feet.

"Why are you here?" Reynolds demanded.

The gurgled response was unintelligible.

"Tell me!"

The male's eyes rolled back in his head, and bloody bubbles around his destroyed mouth marked his last breath.

Reynolds groaned, angry at himself for failing to capture any of the aliens. He already regretted the violence of his last punch, but it was done. They'd have to capture the Loranian ship instead.

The one thing he wouldn't regret was saving the children's lives. When he went back to the teacher on the ground, he found that she was still holding on.

He tore a strip of cloth from his uniform and started binding the teacher's shoulder and back. A cluster of Krokans emerged from the nearby buildings and hurried over.

The people were shy and afraid of him, but they swarmed out to aid the teacher and the kids. He eased back to let them, understanding they could do more than he could.

A short female, barely a wisp who might blow away if the wind were too strong, stepped up to Reynolds and planted her feet in front of him.

For all her frailness, there was a strength that practically glowed in her eyes as she stared Reynolds down.

"I am Mahd Si," she told him, proffering her hand. "We are in your debt, off-worlder."

Reynolds shook his head. "You can call me Reynolds,

and you don't owe me, or anyone for that matter, anything," he answered.

He hated the idea that his and the crew's presence had put these people at risk even more than they usually were. Jiya had been right. Ending slavery was worth the risk and the loss.

The crowd lifted the teacher and gathered the children and swept them away in a bustle of movement. Reynolds watched them go, wishing them luck.

He turned back to Mahd Si after they were gone. "Are you in charge here?"

She chuckled. "As much as any slave can be," she replied with a smile, showing off crooked and badly maintained teeth.

"You're not a slave any longer," he told her, realizing how much he sounded like Jiya, promising something he might not be able to deliver. But it was the right thing to say.

"Is that why you're here?" she asked.

Was it? he wondered.

It might not have been part of the plan, but after seeing the ruin wrought by the Orau, Reynolds was starting to think that maybe freeing these people *was* part of the plan. A strong federation of planets could stand up to the Kurtherians. A Federation. Damn, Bethany Anne was right, too.

"I think it is," he told her, smiling.

There was no way he could leave things the way they were after seeing all they'd been through.

President Jaer Pon might not appreciate Reynolds' generosity when they returned to Krokus 4, but Reynolds didn't give a damn what he thought. The president had sent them there to stop the Orau, and that came with consequences.

Reynolds would see to it that the people on Krokus 1 were taken care of the same as those on Krokus 4.

Better even, seeing how the war footing hadn't been kind to those on Krokus 4.

Regardless, while the SD *Reynolds* and crew were in the system, they would rid it of the Orau and make it so the people could live in peace, without the fear of having their planets raided and razed by pirate scum.

"Can I find you here when I return?" Reynold asked Mahd Si. "I suspect we'll have much to talk about soon."

"I'll have someone keep watch for you." She nodded. "You planning to go after the rest of the Orau?"

Already committed in his head, Reynolds confirmed that was exactly what he planned. "They don't deserve this place," he told her. "It's not theirs, and we'll go after them until we drive them back into the hole out of which they crawled."

"Thank you, Reynolds," she told him, patting him on his arm as if he were one of the children. She offered a soft smile and followed her people without uttering another word.

He wondered for a second what he might be getting himself into, but he knew Bethany Anne would approve of his decision.

In fact, she'd insist on it.

The thought made him smile. Still, there was work to do.

He went over to the bodies of the Loranian crew and crouched to examine them more closely.

He had hated having to kill them all...

Well, he really hadn't hated it, actually.

He had enjoyed killing them, and they had deserved it several times over for their attacks on the superdreadnought and his people.

He'd find out what the crew of the Loranian ship wanted from him eventually.

They'd regret picking him as their target.

Until that time, though, he could still learn a little about his would-be opponents.

Melted Face was the first of the crew he looked at.

In charge, at least until he died, Reynolds figured he'd be the one to carry any mission-sensitive equipment or intel if there was any to be had.

Reynolds searched the body and found a small communication device. He thought about triggering it and taunting the enemy ship's captain into doing something stupid.

Fortunately, the AI understood that calling a battle-ready cruiser down on his head could have negative repercussions.

He was sure the Krokans would appreciate his restraint.

As he went through the pockets and pouches of the melted-faced male, he found nothing of substance beyond the comm device. The armor and weapons were influenced by Kurtherian technology.

Somehow or another the Kurtherians were behind the ship and its mission, whatever it was. Reynolds could come to no other conclusion.

The Kurtherians had had more than one opportunity to come after the superdreadnought, yet they'd been hesitant, working through intermediaries or being careful. Maybe they had already fled the galaxy.

What the hell could they want?

The options were limitless, from wanting Federation tech to needing a captive to use against Bethany Anne and the Federation, to simply wanting Reynolds alive so the Kurtherians could torture him for the hell of it.

Reynolds mentally shrugged. He needed more data to draw a better conclusion before shaping his counterattack strategy.

He went on to search the next body, but there was nothing there. The same was true with the remaining shuttle crew. That didn't mean there wasn't anything he could work with, however.

He memorized the details of the various aliens and examined them for anything—scars, tattoos, markings, whatever—that might set them apart, so he would have the visual information if the opportunity arose to identify them.

That was a long shot, but at least he could research the races they belonged to and possibly find a connection to the Kurtherians or the Loranians. Reynolds would learn what races those were, and they would be next on his list of planets to visit.

With the Loranian crew offering him nothing to ponder, he knew there was little left to do on the planet but wipe out the remaining missile sites, clear out the last of the Orau, and get back to dealing with President Jaer Pon to see what he could do to help the Krokans here on Krokus 1 while also helping those on Krokus 4.

Ready to get on with things, he opened a channel to the superdreadnought.

"Asya! Are you finished playing around up there yet?" he asked. "We'll clean up a few things here and then we're going to need a damn ride back to Krokus 4. I need to have a conversation with Jaer Pon."

"You have the absolute worst timing," Comm replied from the bridge of the *SD Reynolds*.

"Is that Daddy?" Tactical asked. "Tell him to bring pizza for dinner."

"If you continue teasing me with that mystical pizza thing you keep talking about, Tactical, I'm going to shoot you," Asya muttered, watching the viewscreen as the latest sortie of Orau ships closed on them. "It sounds *sooooo* good."

"You have no idea," Tactical told her.

"Exactly," she shot back. "I have no idea, and I want it!"

"If you two are done chatting about dinner, can I get a sitrep?" Reynolds ordered, his voice filling the bridge.

"Six Orau fighter-bombers incoming," Asya reported. "Tactical has taken out most of the launch sites already, only a few left. We've eliminated eighty percent of the missiles, but another wave is already on its way. We have a plan, though."

"Is it a good one?" Reynolds challenged.

Asya chuckled. "I'll let you know in a little while, boss,"

she replied, wondering at the angst in Reynolds' voice. "Takal came up with it."

"Well, at least we know that if it doesn't work, it will be a spectacular failure," Reynolds mumbled.

"What about you?" Asya asked. "You get the shuttle crew sorted?"

"Sorted, twisted, and all but buried," Reynolds answered.

"We have pretty loose operational terms for success, but that doesn't sound much like one to me," Asya told him.

"All depends on the perspective, but we won't be bringing home any captives to interrogate, sadly," the AI reported, disappointment in his voice. "And we still have a number of Orau running around the planet causing trouble, so we're a ways from the finish line on this one."

"Well, as soon as we can spare the shuttle, we'll send it down to collect you," Asya replied, grimacing at the viewscreen. "San Roche is still engaged. Gotta go now, sir. We've got company dropping by."

"Take care of business and maybe we'll find you some of that pizza, Captain Asya," Reynolds replied. "Just don't let Tactical convince you that it needs pineapple on it. Reynolds out." He closed with a laugh as the connection shut down.

"What the hell is pineapple?" Asya asked.

"Fruit of the gods!" Tactical announced.

Further discussion was curtailed by the thunderous rattling of the Orau fighter-bombers engaging the SD *Reynolds*.

"They're on us," Ria reported.

Asya didn't need to comment. Drawing the bombers in close was part of the plan.

"Missiles are rising at their backs," Ria went on.

"Time for you to work your magic," Asya told Takal over the comm.

"This can hardly be considered magic, my dear," he replied. "This is a purely scientific response to a—"

"Just do what you're going to do, or I'll shoot you out the airlock and have you take on the ships by hand, Takal," she sniped.

"On it," the inventor replied. An alarm flashed on her console, clarifying that Takal had fired the pucks into space. "They're away," he reported.

"I know we probably should have discussed this earlier, but how will these things get past the Orau shields?" Asya wondered.

"The pucks are so small, as well as inert in their normal state, that they will pass harmlessly through the shield and attach themselves to the hull without alerting the Orau that it's even happened," Takal explained. "Once they're attached, the trigger devices on them can be activated."

The SD *Reynolds* shuddered under another barrage and Asya snarled at the viewscreen. "These guys are starting to piss me off. Tactical?"

"I also took the liberty of dumping the trash while I was at it," Takal told her.

Asya watched the screen as the ship's debris spilled out into space, trailing the superdreadnought. She thought she caught a glimpse of one of the tiny pucks tumbling alongside the trash.

The Orau ships flew right into the mess before veering off.

Takal's laughter flooded over the speakers. "It's like fishing for morons," he said. "I've eight confirmed latches on three of the Orau ships."

"Trigger those, Takal," Asya ordered, then twisted in her seat to glance at Tactical's position.

Although she always felt stupid doing it, she felt it best to address the post, even if the AI's personality wasn't actually in it.

"Target the three that don't have hitchhikers and keep them too busy to get above us," she called. "XO, shift energy to lower shields and make ready for missile impacts. Ria, bring us about to block as many of the missile paths as possible, belly up."

The crew leapt to do as commanded. Asya hoped she was making the right choice.

"Pucks ignited," Takal called. Asya was happy to see the enemy fighter-bombers leaking sparks.

With no atmosphere, the sparks died as soon as they started to flare, but Takal had assured that they didn't need to see the discharged elements for them to work.

And sure enough, he was right.

As the salvo of missiles closed, she could see an immediate reaction on the scanners.

The missiles nearest the tagged Orau veered off course erratically, almost as if their targeting systems had been fried by a massive EMP. Their engines drove them relentlessly.

The first of the tagged Orau didn't notice the change and was rear-ended by a half-dozen missiles.

The ship exploded, shrapnel and debris destroying other missiles in its wake.

Ria cheered, but Asya hunkered down, keeping her eyes on the viewscreen. They weren't out of the fight yet.

Several missiles struck the shields of the *Reynolds*, their reverberation shaking the massive ship as they impacted. The gravitic shields held.

A second Orau ship tried to avoid the missiles, but Tactical's constant weapons fire pushed it dead into the path. The Orau was dust and debris a moment later.

Asya spied a few missiles explode on their own and zoomed in to see that they had impacted the pucks directly, the magnetic clamps drawing them in and detonating the warheads.

Tactical whooped as he blew one of the Orau ships away, then focused his efforts on the others.

"Damn it!" XO cried. "We've got one of the Orau slipping over the top of us."

"I got it!" Ria shot back.

Not to be outdone in the fight, the young ensign pushed the SD *Reynolds* forward and up, swinging the nose about as though it were a giant boot heel squashing a bug.

It was just as effective.

The shields caught the Orau vessel before it could dodge and the ship was slammed backward, spinning out of control until it exploded.

Tactical shot down another and another until there were none left.

Free of the Orau bombers, Tactical, Helm, and San Roche were able to focus on the remaining missiles while Asya targeted the last of the launch sites.

As the final one disappeared from the scanners, she slumped into her seat and grinned. "Excellent work, people," she told them. "Now let's get our crew back aboard, San Roche."

The shuttle pilot replied in the affirmative, and the shuttle dropped from near orbit on its way to the planet's surface to collect the crew.

Asya smiled and let her head loll against the headrest of her seat.

"Somebody owes us pizza, damn it."

CHAPTER NINETEEN

Back aboard the superdreadnought, Reynolds surveyed his kingdom.

"Doesn't look too much worse for wear," he said after a quiet moment. "Excellent work, people."

"Did you expect anything less?" Tactical asked.

"You really want an answer to that?" Reynolds fired back.

"Mission accomplished, it looks like," Asya interjected. She figured it was time for Tactical to take a break.

"Not quite yet," Jiya replied, shaking her head.

"What am I missing?" Asya wondered.

"It turns out there are still a large number of Orau soldiers dirtside who need to be dealt with."

"How are we supposed to do that?" Asya asked. "It's not like they're going to sit still and let us shoot them."

"Already in motion," Reynolds told her with a sly grin. "Comm, open a channel for me." Reynolds provided a specific frequency, and Comm did as ordered.

"Channel's connecting," Comm announced.

"You made friends while you were down there?" Asya asked.

Reynolds grinned. "I'm a charmer, what can I say?"

"You there, Mahd Si?" Reynolds asked.

The old female's soft voice came back right away. "I am indeed, Reynolds."

"Were you able to do as we discussed?" Reynolds asked.

While he was stuck dirtside waiting to be collected, an idea had struck him. He reached out to Mahd Si and organized a surprise for the surviving Orau on Krokus 1.

"Exactly as you requested," Mahd Si replied.

"Excellent," Reynolds told her. "Have your people hunker down, and my crew and I will take care of your infestation problem."

She laughed softly. "Execute your plan, Reynolds and may the Krokan god smile on you and your crew."

"I'm sorry we don't have room to haul all of you back to Krokus 4 with us, but I promise I'll negotiate terms with President Jaer Pon and get supplies to you or an agreement for relocation, whatever works best for you and your people."

"You're a saint, Reynolds," Mahd Si told him.

"Awwwwwww," the crew intoned as one, amused smiles all around.

"We'll talk soon, Mahd Si," Reynolds closed. "Be careful. Reynolds out."

The AI cut the link, and Tactical laughed at him.

"Looks like you made one hell of an impression down there, Reynolds," Tactical said. "You give her a peek under the chassis while you were at it?"

"I'm going to put my foot in *your* chassis if you keep it up," Reynolds fired back.

"Don't threaten me with a good time," Tactical told him, chuckling.

Jiya stepped in right then, playing the mediator. "What are your orders, sir?"

Reynolds noted she only called him sir when she was mad or when she wanted him to get on with things.

"Bring up a scan of the outpost," he told her.

Jiya did, and her eyes narrowed at what she saw. "That's...odd."

"It looks like there's a mass migration going on down there," Asya reported, leaning over Jiya's shoulder and examining the screen. "Are those Krokans?"

"Scanners say it's the Orau," Jiya said, eyes wide with disbelief. "What would make them pull out like that?" She glanced at Reynolds.

"Maybe someone made them an offer they couldn't refuse," Reynolds replied.

Jiya nodded. She wished Reynolds had shared his plan. She'd been insubordinate enough on this mission alone to rate being treated like a second-class crewmember. She held her tongue for a private conversation with Reynolds where she would try to convince him of her commitment and professionalism.

She'd been committed to his mission since she'd agreed to leave her home behind, but she hadn't been professional. She'd been a sniveling child who let emotions guide her actions.

No more.

"I asked Mahd Si to have one of her people drop off the

communication device I found on the shuttle crew where it would be found by the Orau.

"It's been transmitting a regular message *from* the assholes on the Loranian ship…" he put air quotes around the word "from," "telling them we've left the system and the ships are coming back to pick them *all* up to transfer them to another planet where they still have resources."

"And they bought it?" Tactical asked. "Fucking morons."

Reynolds nodded. "They've spent a lot of time around Mahd Si and her people and they apparently have big mouths, always talking about things they shouldn't." Reynolds grinned, thinking about the conversation. "While I didn't get the name of the head honcho aboard the Loranian ship, I did get the name of the Orau's contact and enough other pertinent information to make the message sound authentic."

The AI gestured to the screen as evidence.

"Looks like it worked," Jiya said.

"So, you pranked them into a barbeque without anyone bringing the meat?" Tactical asked. "How's that going to— Oooh."

Reynolds grinned. "Oooh, indeed."

Jiya and Asya got it at the same time, both smiling.

"Do what you do best," Reynolds told Tactical.

"Better yet," Jiya interrupted, "how about you just blow them up instead?"

"You take all the fun out of innuendo, Jiya," Tactical complained, but he didn't hold back with the weapon systems.

The *Reynolds'* railguns came online and Tactical unleashed them on the Orau gathered below. Hitting the planet at hypervelocity had the same effect as if the *Reynolds* had dropped a tactical nuke on their heads. The surrounding buildings suffered greatly, but they were the ones the Orau had confiscated.

The bridge crew watched the main screen as the blips of bad guys went poof. He wished he could have been there in person to see it, but they had other things to take care of right then.

Reynolds signaled to Ria.

"Get us back to Krokus 4, Ensign," he ordered. "We have a president to settle up with."

"Course plotted, sir," Ria replied.

A moment later, they were on their way.

If the crew had expected to return as conquering heroes, they were disappointed.

Minister To Gul met them at the landing field and led them in silence to a private presidential compound different from the one they had stayed at before.

"Bit of a change from last time, don't you think?" Jiya whispered to Reynolds as the minister led the crew into the meeting hall.

In the room were nearly fifty of the presidential guards, lining both walls, weapons in hand. President Jaer Pon and Vice President Shal Ura were there, as were Flor and Sergeant Gib.

The administrative pair sat in what looked to be rather uncomfortable chairs, and it showed in their moods.

Both looked anxious and unhappy.

The vice president brightened perceptibly at their arrival, but Jaer Pon simply stared with cold eyes.

"This can't be good," Reynolds muttered, and Jiya nodded in agreement.

Ka'nak, Geroux, and San Roche followed a few steps behind Reynolds and Jiya, none of them wanting to become a part of the conversation that followed.

"What's with the long faces?" Reynolds asked.

The minister huffed at his lack of decorum, but the vice president didn't seem to care. She rose and walked over to the crew. Jaer Pon reluctantly followed her.

"It appears there was an attempt on your lives while you were gone," she stated.

Ka'nak twitched, one eye closing. "I'm not a math wizard, but that doesn't add up. How could someone try to kill us when we weren't here?"

"They obviously failed," Shal Ura replied matter-of-factly.

Jiya rubbed her temple, looking as if she might have an aneurysm. "Would you explain, please?"

The president motioned to one of his guards, who collected a body from a curtained alcove, dropping the corpse at the feet of the crew.

"This is one of the people who broke into the compound and assaulted your room while you were away." He turned and glared at the vice president. "Obviously, no harm was done since you were not here, and my people have dealt with them already."

"It's not as simple as that, Mister President," Shal Ura argued, but the president was having none.

He waved a hand for her to be quiet. "It *is* as simple as that, Shal. Now, please let me speak with our guests."

Reynolds and Jiya exchanged looks. There was something more going on than the president was letting on, but Reynolds didn't figure he'd get a chance to quiz the VP about it without Jaer Pon around to police her.

She glared for a moment, then spun on her heel and marched back to her chair and flopped into it sullenly. Flor set a reassuring hand on Jiya's shoulder. A handful of guards edged closer, including the sergeant.

Once she was seated, Jaer Pon let out an exaggerated sigh. "We can speak bluntly at last."

The first officer bit back a snarl, her demeanor wrestling with her instinct to lash out. She won, holding her anger at bay. The vice president was right there and could hear Jaer Pon being an ass.

"What's going on?" Reynolds asked, not wanting to get into the politics unless he absolutely had to.

"Your mission on Krokus 1...was it successful?" the president asked. "We were struck by perhaps a dozen missiles earlier and feared you had been defeated."

Reynolds shook his head. "We cleared the whole planet of Orau, and that includes their launch sites," he reported. "There won't be any further attacks from Krokus 1, I promise."

"Excellent! Excellent!" Jaer Pon crowed, clapping his hands.

"Our success there opens up another matter regarding the planet, though," Reynolds said, interrupting his cheer.

A curious eyebrow rose on Jaer Pon's face. "And that matter is?"

"As I'm sure you were aware, and simply forgot to inform us, there are people living on the planet—fellow Krokans."

Jaer Pon stiffened. Reynolds had inserted the verbal knife. Now to twist it.

"Thanks to the scavenging Orau," Reynolds went on, "these people are in desperate need of supplies and equipment and a total rebuild of their infrastructure."

Reynolds had initially thought to request that President Jaer Pon migrate the other Krokans to Krokus 4, but thought better of it. They were better off governing themselves.

Best if the Krokans stay independent and live their lives where they are, he thought.

"Given the miscommunication between our two sides, I'd like to amend our agreement. The cost of the defense ring now includes the maintenance and care of the people of Krokus 1, at least until they get back on their feet."

"That's perhaps a tad excessive," Jaer Pon argued.

"So was sending us off to do your dirty work with the Orau without fully informing us of the operational situation," Reynolds fired back.

He was pissed at the president and wasn't going to sugarcoat his feelings for the sake of diplomacy.

While he would be disappointed—or rather, Takal would be—if they left the planet without the schematics for the water purification system, Reynolds was more than willing to sacrifice that advance to make it clear to Jaer Pon that the SD *Reynolds* and its crew would not be used as puppets.

"I-I…" the president started, then offered a conciliatory

nod. "You're right, I was not as clear regarding the situation as I should have been. My apologies."

Reynolds nodded his acceptance of the president's apology, but he caught sight of the vice president sneering across the room. Close enough to have heard them, he wondered if she was reacting to what was being said or if she was still pissed at the president. Reynolds figured it was the latter when her glare settled firmly on Jaer Pon's back.

Reynolds wondered if the president could feel it.

He sure could.

"There was more to our situation than politics allowed me to share, Reynolds," Jaer Pon went on. "To that point, I, too, must ask for an adjustment to our agreement."

Reynolds heard Jiya tapping her fingers on her thigh, and he knew without looking that the first officer was giving the president the same glare as the vice president.

"How...unexpected," Reynolds remarked, his tone and expression making it clear it wasn't.

Jaer Pon went on as if he hadn't noticed.

Reynolds was quite sure he had.

The president gestured at the body on the floor. It was a Krokan.

"This terrorist was part of a group that supports the Orau and its goals of taking over Krokus 4, the Knights of Orau. There are quite a number of them on our planet, believe it or not, and they are largely to blame for the unrest that has plagued us and brought our great people down. Were their leader to be killed, however, they would fall apart."

Reynolds stared at Jaer Pon, trying to figure out

whether he was lying, but the president was a true politician. That guaranteed he *was* lying, but about what exactly, no one could be sure. He sold it perfectly, even if it didn't make sense.

"So, a political enemy of yours took a shot at us to get at you?" Jiya asked. "Why would they do that and what concern is that of ours?"

"Because rumors have been spread that you are here to rid us of our Knights problem," Jaer Pon replied. "They will do anything to protect themselves, and killing off-worlders does nothing to harm their status with the people."

"I wonder how those rumors started?" Jiya mused, keeping her voice even.

To Reynolds' surprise, she didn't push any harder, leaving Reynolds to discuss the matter with the president.

"So, these Knights…" Reynolds let the subject hang for a moment before finishing his thought. "You know where we can find them, I presume?"

"I do indeed," Jaer Pon answered, the barest flicker of a smile playing at his lips. "We have quite a bit of intel on them, although we are not well-equipped to do more than minimize their attempts at tearing our society apart from within."

"So you want us to do it for you?" Reynolds asked matter-of-factly. "Kill their leader and shut the Knights down?"

"We would be indebted to you, Reynolds," Jaer Pon replied.

"No, you will be indebted to the people of Krokus 1," the AI corrected. "We'll do this for them, for sufficient supplies, equipment, and credits to get them back on their feet. Are we agreed?"

Although the president looked as if he'd just bitten into a rancid lemon, he nodded.

"Yes, if you slay the leader of the Knights and bring her head to me, then we are agreed," he said. "I will have Minister To Gul provide you with all the intelligence you need on the Knights, and I look forward to seeing you and your crew succeed."

The president nodded and spun on his heel, leaving the room with an entourage of guards, Flor and Sergeant Gib following.

The vice president rose to her feet, wanting to come over and speak to Reynolds, but Minister To Gul ushered the crew out before she could make her way past her guards. They left before anyone could intercept them and provide an alternate version of reality.

The minister led them to a small room and left them to speak with a senior guard who had all the details they needed.

As soon as the intel had been passed on, they were sent on their way unceremoniously to get to work.

Out in the hall with just the crew around, Jiya turned to Reynolds. He could see the doubt and disgust in her eyes.

"Are we doing this…again?" she asked, not condemning but clarifying.

"Don't think of it as being for the president. Think of it as us doing a good deed for the people of the planet."

"And you believe that?"

"Not really," Reynolds answered, "but it gives us an

opportunity to further explore this planet and interact with its people to see if we can figure out what's going on."

"Or what's *not* going on," Geroux clarified.

Reynolds shrugged. "Either works, but there's more to this situation than they're letting on, and I am free to modify the arrangement if we can prove the president is lying."

"You mean like President Weasel using us as his personal military force to clean up all the opposition to his rule?" Jiya asked. "There's something wrong with that, Reynolds. Are we just going to buy into it?"

"The only thing we're buying into is the opportunity to see what's really going on," the AI returned. "Right now, the Orau are clearly the bad guys here, even if they turn out to not be the only ones. They were subjugating the people of Krokus 1 and making their lives hell, not to mention bombarding the people of Krokus 4. As such, we're on the side of right…so far."

"I still feel as if we're being manipulated," Jiya complained.

"Me too," Geroux added.

Ka'nak grunted and San Roche had nothing to say, shrugging when they looked in his direction.

"I'm not saying he isn't trying to manipulate us, Jiya. To the contrary. I know he is, but there are partial truths that we are now free to explore. We know that the people in this system need our help," Reynolds told her. "If that means we play bad cop to root out the even worse cops, I'm all for it."

"I'm not sure what a cop is, but I get the gist of what you mean," Jiya answered.

"Then you know we're going into this with our eyes open," Reynolds went on. "The Orau demonstrated that they deserved their fate, and if these guys *are* affiliated with them, then they too deserve what's coming to them."

After the crew left the compound, Reynolds gestured to the surrounding area.

As before, the war-torn aspects of it stood out plainly.

"Look at this place," Reynolds told her. "These people need a break from the fight. If Jaer Pon is part of the problem, we'll find that out. We're obligated to look into it, at the very least."

Jiya nodded. "I agree. I just don't want us being used against the people. This guy is playing us. I just don't know to what end."

"Control? Power?" Ka'nak suggested. "These guys are all the same."

"He's not wrong," Geroux agreed.

"Well then, we learn what we can while we track down this information," Reynolds temporized. "If something comes up that we don't agree with, we'll cross that bridge when we come to it. Until that time, let's chase these leads."

The crew grunted their agreement and Reynolds started off again.

He was just as suspicious as the crew about Jaer Pon's motives, but as Ka'nak suggested, it could simply be an effort on the president's part to maintain his rule. The way he shut down the vice president spoke of him wanting to be in charge and remain there.

Maybe that was all it was.

If it wasn't, Reynolds had no problem changing the deal by removing Jaer Pon from power.

CHAPTER TWENTY

Ready to go after the Knights of Orau, the crew made their way through town, following the directions provided to them by the president's people.

The intel had led them to a crappy corner of town, where Jiya could picture the bad guys hiding or lurking.

Or...the poor.

She scoffed as she surveyed the area from her position hunkered atop a ramshackle building that swayed with nearly every gust of artificial wind.

Geroux, Ka'nak, and Reynolds were there with her. They'd sent San Roche back to the shuttle since he'd turned out to be a solid backup, what Reynolds called "the cavalry."

The Telluride seemed content to do whatever was asked of him, and Jiya knew she'd have to break him of that eventually. He would have to let go of the slave mentality he'd brought with him from Grindlevik 3.

It was one thing to serve a crew and be a part of a team,

but they didn't need a yes person. They needed a partner and a team member, someone they could count on to stand firm and hold his ground. She needed to make sure he was thinking as a free crewman and not a slave blindly following orders.

She knew he and L'Eliana would make great additions to the crew. They just needed a little seasoning.

Jiya suspected she'd get a little bit more herself by going after the Knights.

People traipsed about in the streets below now and again, but few had passed the building in which Jaer Pon's people had indicated the Knights made their headquarters.

Seeing the old, broken-down building brought back her distrust of the president.

Set at the very edge of the energy field that separated the town from the vastness of the ocean, she couldn't see how the place could contain more than a couple dozen people, let alone enough to challenge all the guards she'd seen the president sporting.

Jiya figured a brick thrown hard enough at the place would collapse it. In fact, the building looked so precarious that Jiya began to wonder if the president wanted them to go inside, figuring it would fall on their heads and remove them without him having to do anything.

"This must be Jaer Pon's vacation home," Ka'nak joked, staring at the ramshackle hulk. "I wonder if there's a pool."

"Yeah," Jiya replied. "It's about twenty paces that way." She pointed at the wall of energy that kept the ocean from crashing in and wiping the town away.

"Beachfront property," Ka'nak muttered. "Nice."

"Dump a pound of sand at the back door, and that's exactly what you'd have," Reynolds told him.

Jiya could tell the AI wasn't feeling any better about the mission than she was, although he'd done his best to motivate her for it.

Then again, that was his job.

Yet, at the end of the day, she felt used, and she was pretty damn sure that kicking in the door of this place and rousting its occupants wasn't going to make her feel any better about what they were doing or for whom.

"You sure this is the right address?" Geroux asked. She glanced at the computer on her wrist, examining the screen. "I'm not seeing anything but the barest source of electricity running through the place. If this is some supervillain's hideout, I don't think we have anything to worry about."

"The Orau weren't exactly sophisticated, but these guys look like bargain-basement bad guys," Jiya said.

"This is the location," Reynolds confirmed. "They're supposed to be keeping a low profile."

"Doesn't get much lower than this," Ka'nak confirmed, "Except, of course, for the whole part about us being led right to the front door and all."

Jiya held her tongue and tried to appear sympathetic, but Reynolds gave her a look, telling her that he understood the group's argument and nothing was going to change.

She smiled and nodded, acquiescing. The captain's decision was final, and it was her job to see it carried out.

"What do you need us to do?" she asked, continuing when he didn't answer quickly enough, "Since we didn't get solid numbers on how many of the Knights are here normally, how do you want to do this?"

"I'm thinking—"

"About time you people got back," Maddox's voice cut across the comm, interrupting them. "I figured you'd left the system and forgot me."

"We would never do that," Ka'nak assured him, tapping the comm implant in the side of his head while mouthing, "Who's this?"

"Good to hear from you, General." Reynolds ignored the Melowi warrior. "Been a little busy since we returned," he said by way of explanation for them forgetting to contact the one they'd left behind. Jiya's mouth fell open in shock.

They *had* forgotten. Every last one of them, even the AI with the impeccable memory.

"Understand," Maddox came back skeptically. "Been a little busy myself. I've got a story to tell, one that starts with, 'No shit, there I was…' but I'll skip to the juicy bits."

Reynolds stiffened, curiosity obvious in his expression. "What's going on?"

"Well, I witnessed an attempt on our lives, although that didn't work out too well for our would-be assassins."

"So I heard," Reynolds replied. "Go on."

"I followed a couple of the survivors from the compound and managed to collect one of them alive. He and I have spent a little while together already, but he's not very talkative. Of course, that probably has something to do with him still being unconscious and all, but I've learned that whoever wants us dead is called Phraim-'Eh.

There's also some master who wasn't named, so we're apparently looking at more than one person."

Reynolds froze. *Phraim-'Eh*. It was not a name that would randomly appear. That was one of the Kurtherian clans.

"Where are you?" Reynolds asked, excitement in his voice. "I need to see this hostage of yours."

The general gave his location and Reynolds cut the link, promising to be right there. He hopped to his feet.

"Change of plan," he started.

Jiya caught him by the arm before he could take off. "You want us to go too?"

Reynolds shook his head.

"No, go forward with the mission," he told her. "Observe before you act. Find someone to talk to before you breach the building. See what you can learn from the people inside, but do your best not to hurt anyone."

He said nothing else, running to the location Maddox had given him.

"So, here we are again," Ka'nak said with a grin. "I say we go knock some heads together."

Jiya sighed. "You heard him. Gather more info before going in," she told the warrior. "We're not going to hurt anyone, not until we're sure who's on whose side."

"If these guys attack us when we go down there we'll know whose side they're on," Ka'nak explained.

"You mean after we randomly kick in their door and raid their home?" Geroux asked.

"Exactly," Ka'nak agreed. "Now you're thinking like a warrior."

Jiya chuckled. "How about we knock on the door and

go from there, no kicking it or asses until we figure things out."

"We might as well bring flowers while we're at it," the Melowi complained. "Maybe some cookies."

"Neither's a bad idea," Geroux agreed, grinning. "Starts this off on the right foot, I think. Only enemies would attack someone carrying cookies or flowers."

Ka'nak groaned. "I should have gone with the AI. At least he's going to throw down."

"The day's still young, Ka'nak," Jiya told him. "Plenty of time left to bust heads."

He sighed. "You're the boss."

"I am, and I'll do my best to carry out Reynolds' orders," Jiya confirmed, stretching to work out the kinks before she and the crew headed downstairs on their way to the house.

As much as she hoped there'd be a roadmap to a conspiracy posted on the door of the Knights' building, she knew there wouldn't be. There would be misinformation, confusion, redirection, running, yelling, and it would probably end in a fight.

Didn't it always?

With that thought in her head, they continued down the path that she saw had only one conclusion.

Once outside, they surveyed the scene and started across the road when they were sure there was no one to witness their approach.

Geroux had already assessed that there were no cameras nearby and there was nothing that constituted a sophisticated alarm or security system on the building. Technology was nonexistent.

Worst evil lair ever. Or the best. Jiya couldn't decide which.

Up close, it was precisely what it looked like: a ruin amidst more ruins.

This part of town had been bombed out by the Orau and largely abandoned, which made its choice as the Knights' hideout even more suspect to her.

There was no hiding out here, no fading into a crowd and losing tails. No, it was block after block of dilapidated buildings with so little foot traffic that the presence of anyone on the streets made them stand out.

Like they did as they crossed into the shadows of the building and eased against the wall.

"I don't like this," Geroux mumbled.

Neither did Jiya, but what choice did they have?

She acknowledged her friend's feelings with a shallow nod and moved to the door. She didn't even need to check if it was locked.

It swung open with a *creak* as she neared it, the uneven flooring popping it open with her weight.

"That's not ominous at all," Geroux complained.

Jiya motioned for Ka'nak to go first.

He grinned and started in.

"No head-busting," she reminded. "Not unless it's necessary."

"It's always necessary," he said as he slipped inside.

Jiya grunted and followed, Geroux at her side. The smell of mildew and salt struck them almost immediately.

Geroux wrinkled her nose at the stench and Jiya breathed through her mouth to keep from inhaling too much.

"Smells like the ocean is reclaiming lost territory," Ka'nak whispered as they moved deeper into the apparently empty house.

Jiya had to agree. Although her experience with oceans was minimal, she recognized the smell from her childhood. She had wondered at the time why in the hell people wanted to hang out somewhere that stank of dead fish and dirty water.

That had been the last time her mother had taken her to see the ocean.

She sighed at the memory, pushing it aside as the crew crept farther into the rundown house, the smell leading the way.

"It's this way," Ka'nak said, pointing down a flight of rickety stairs.

He started down without a word, stepping wide and planting his feet at the edges of the steps, making sure to put his weight where the supports were the strongest.

Jiya followed his example and pointed to make sure Geroux did, too.

The stairs creaked even with the precautions, but they held despite Jiya's expectation that they would collapse.

They turned out to be stronger than they looked.

At the bottom, Jiya heard a pair of muffled voices, and Ka'nak raised a closed fist to bring them to a halt. Jiya eased closer to listen as the voices carried on without interruption.

"You're certain of this?" one asked, that of a female.

"We've been given little choice, Val," a male replied, his voice raspy and deep.

"That doesn't make it right, Ko," the female argued.

"Maybe not, but our back's against the wall," the male returned. "Jaer Pon has made sure of that."

Jiya stiffened, hearing the president's name. She inched forward, desperate to hear something that might exonerate or convict the pair of speakers; something she could use to base her decision on as to whether to act.

"We can't have these off-worlders tearing apart everything we've worked for," the male went on.

"Who says they will?" the female asked.

"You saw what happened at the compound," the male fired back. "There's no way—"

"I think you've heard just about enough," a different voice said, the sound of a weapon being charged emphasizing the cold touch of the barrel on Jiya's temple.

She froze, her eyes darting sideways. The person who held her at gunpoint wasn't alone.

Five people stood beside him, each with a pistol pointed at the crew. Locals, she realized immediately.

She recognized one of them from the fight when Sergeant Gib had led them to the secret enclave of the rich and petty.

"I know you," she said.

He pressed his gun harder against her head. "You know nothing."

"Easy," said another local who'd slipped into the room while they'd been distracted. A female stood next to him, and Jiya presumed these were Val and Ko.

Ka'nak looked ready to pounce.

Wait, she said over the mental link. She didn't need the Melowi shedding blood.

Not yet, at least.

227

"More of the president's spies," another of them said, this one older and scarred.

"We're hardly spies," Jiya argued.

The one holding the gun to her head chuckled at that. "Clearly, since we heard you approaching the instant you opened the door."

"If you're not spies, then why are you here?" Val asked, hands on her hips. She wore a strange suit of oiled skin that clung to her firm figure.

Ko wore something similar, as did the people surrounding them. Jiya could smell the ocean on them.

"Jaer Pon *did* send us here—" Jiya started.

"I warned you," the older male shouted, letting out a growl.

"Relax, Tog," Ko told him.

"How can I relax when you're leaving their weapons on them like that?" Tog ranted, nearly frothing at the mouth.

"He's right." Jiya eased her hands into the air, making it clear she wasn't trying to do anything aggressive. "Take our weapons," she told them. "We're not here to hurt you."

"This is a bad idea," Ka'nak snarled.

"Maybe," Jiya shot back, "but let them have your gun."

The Melowi growled as the people took their weapons away. He held his ground, eyes assessing each. Jiya knew he was planning how to kill each and every one of those in the room.

Jiya swallowed a sigh of relief that he didn't act.

With the pistol pressed to her temple, she knew that any resistance would end with a smoking hole in her skull.

Not exactly how she wanted to finish her day.

Besides, she was sure these people weren't who President Jaer Pon claimed they were.

"You're not the Knights of the Orau, are you?" she asked.

The person with the gun to her head laughed and pulled it away, although he still aimed it in her direction.

"Knights of the what?" he asked.

"Orau," Geroux clarified. "It's who we were told was operating out of this building."

The local grinned widely. "If those so-called Knights live here, we need to start charging the bastards rent."

"The only place they're living is in the head of Jaer Pon," Ko stated, shaking his head. He looked at Val. "I told you about what happened at the compound. Why would the cultists go after these people unless they were a threat to the president? He had to have hired them."

"Wait," Jiya said, turning to face Ko. "You think the president sent the assassins after us?"

"Assassins?" Tog asked, laughing, the sound rough, like two rocks grinding together. "I'd hardly call that lot of malcontents assassins."

"I'm confused," Geroux said.

"You're not the only one," Jiya mumbled, looking at the people surrounding them and Ko and Val.

"Why don't you explain it, Roe?" Ko suggested, gesturing to the person who had held his gun to Jiya's head.

"I don't think it's my place to do so," he countered, "but I'm thinking Lek would want to meet these folks in person."

"Lek?" Ka'nak asked.

"Our leader," Val explained.

"Yeah, how about you give him a call?" Jiya said, hoping to buy some time to figure everything out.

The Krokans laughed at her, Roe shaking his head, eyes bright with amusement.

"Lek's not somebody you call," he answered, although Jiya noted he didn't explain why not.

"You think this is a good idea?" Ko asked.

"Lek'll let us know soon enough," Roe replied. "Get these folks suited up."

"Suited up?" Jiya asked. "I don't understand."

Roe gestured to their armor. "Well, you can't go into the water wearing that."

"Not unless you're looking to drown," Tog added with a laugh.

"I guess we're taking a swim, then," Jiya muttered.

While it was better than being shot, this wasn't how she'd imagined ending her day either.

But if that was where the mission took her, so be it. Reynolds had said to get information without hurting anyone.

Now more than ever, she wanted to know what the hell was going on in this crazy underwater city.

"The water's not going to smell like dead fish, is it?" she asked.

Roe chuckled. "Only if you take a really deep breath."

Jiya didn't smile, activating her implant instead and keeping her message short. *We're being taken by the building's inhabitants into the ocean. They've never heard of the Knights. No locals were harmed in the creation of this message.*

Good job. Keep me informed, Reynolds replied before cutting the link.

CHAPTER TWENTY-ONE

Jora'nal paced the bridge of the *Pillar*, his fury still raging.

He'd chased his crew away, except for a few key members. They knew to keep their distance and let him vent his anger in the fits and tirades that helped him calm himself.

With no one but himself to blame for the failure to recognize that the SD *Reynolds* had been orbiting Krokus 1 or the defeat he suffered at their hands, he'd forced everyone off the bridge to keep from killing someone he might need at a later time.

Besides, the deck was beginning to retain the sickly color of blood no matter how much effort the crew had put into cleaning it.

So many people had died on their knees before him.

Normally, the memories of each punishing moment would sustain him and invigorate him, but not today. No, today he had failed and would have to stand before the Voice to explain himself.

It was not a task he relished, since it could very well be him staining the deck with his blood; Phraim-'Eh asking for the ultimate sacrifice of his disciple.

Jora'nal prayed that would not come to pass, but could he blame his master, were that to be his punishment?

No, he didn't think he could, especially given the number of lives that had ended at his hands.

"Incoming contact," XO H'ron announced from his place across the bridge.

Jora'nal drew a deep breath and despised the way it tasted. Would it be his last?

"Onscreen," he ordered.

There was little point in delaying. If Phraim-'Eh wanted him dead, that was simply how it would be. There was no place in the universe where he would be safe from his god's righteous vengeance.

The face of the Voice of Phraim-'Eh appeared on the screen. Although Jora'nal could not read anything his stoic expression, hard lines staring back, Jora'nal felt the disappointment across the vast expanse of space.

"Master," Jora'nal said reverently, bowing his head and waiting for the Voice to speak.

"I can only hope your failure here is not going to become a habit, Jora'nal," the Voice told him.

"No, Master. A setback, nothing more," Jora'nal explained.

He hated the sound of his groveling voice, but he knew well the consequences of displeasing Phraim-'Eh and those who served the god.

"Let that be true, for our god is not a merciful one, lest you have forgotten," the Voice went on.

"I have not, Master, and this will not happen again," Jora'nal assured his deity's mouthpiece. "We have agents on the ground with the Federation scum, working to bring them down. We will have them soon enough."

The Voice nodded, leaving the threat of his silence hanging in the air a moment.

"An agent of our god will be in touch soon, Jora'nal," the Voice revealed. "You and they might well find solace in your mutual cause, and possibly inspiration as well."

"Yes, Master," Jora'nal answered, bowing.

"Continue your mission, and I will relay your thoughts to our lord."

The screen flickered, and the image of the Voice of Phraim-'Eh vanished into blackness.

Jora'nal staggered back to his seat, dropping into it hard.

Not only had he disappointed his god, but now another agent of Phraim-'Eh had been put into play.

The fact that this agent was to meet with Jora'nal sent a chill down his spine. There was no secret to this agent's agenda.

What other reason is there but to kill me?

No, Jora'nal thought, shaking off his fear. Phraim-'Eh needed no such mundane subterfuge to achieve his will. He need only to ask Jora'nal to take his own life and he would, willingly, like a zealot at the gates of the great beyond.

No, if Phraim-'Eh wanted Jora'nal to meet this agent, it was because their goals collided, crossed paths, and their meeting would compound the suffering the Federation AI Reynolds was to suffer at their hands.

A thrill set his blood alight and he straightened in his

seat, grinning. "Set a course for Ol'fer Prime," he ordered. "There is much to be done to the *Pillar* before we meet the SD *Reynolds* in battle again."

This time it will not be the Pillar *that flees,* he thought.

CHAPTER TWENTY-TWO

Jiya was both excited and terrified by the massive ocean that enveloped her.

The Krokans had provided skintight suits and a breathing apparatus for the crew, which was built into the narrow helmet she'd squeezed her head into.

Geroux had argued fearfully about the pressure of the water but the Krokans had laughed her off, assuring her the suits would sustain them. Geroux hadn't been sure until Val explained how each generated its own personal energy field, much like the one that surrounded the city and kept the ocean at bay.

Although the smaller field didn't keep the water out, it did keep the pressure from crushing them into a bloody pulp inside their suits.

Jiya wasn't confident that would be the case when they were loaded into a room that looked as if it were an air bubble—much like the craft that had brought them to the city—and the door had sealed behind them.

The tiny room looked out into the ocean, and the sharp contrast of a wall of water and the dilapidated house on the other side was jarring.

The same was true of her senses.

One minute she could smell the briny water, the trademark stink of the ocean, then the bubble opened and the ocean rushed in to swallow her whole.

Then she could smell and hear nothing.

The pressure of the water grabbed her and squeezed and she tightened her muscles against it, knowing there was nothing she could do to prevent the water from crushing her if that were its desire.

Yet it didn't.

It buoyed her, lifted her along with the others. She felt light and weightless, as if the whole world floated around her.

Roe waved at her and kicked free of the bubble, slipping into the vast depths of the ocean. The others followed, but it took a moment before Jiya chased after them.

Roe pulled Geroux with her as they slipped into the water, bumping into something she couldn't quite make out in the blur of her vision.

She saw Roe grin and extend a hand to them.

A moment later he pulled them onto what appeared to be a platform made of glass, though Jiya knew that couldn't be the case.

It was clear—see-through to the point of being almost invisible—yet it was physically there. She could feel it beneath her feet, the solidness of it.

Then it started moving.

Ka'nak dropped onto his ass with wide eyes peering

into the deep. Tog steadied him, but the Melowi warrior remained where he sat.

Jiya wanted to laugh, but she knew damn well her face was making the same pained, ugly grimace as his.

Geroux trembled against Jiya, but the young tech looked like her uncle Takal right then. Her face hid the fear, reflecting only her urge to learn and experience the moment and study the technology that made it all possible.

She was taking it in as if they were on some sort of pleasure cruise.

Maybe we are, Jiya thought.

She was still quite confused, but she thought things were beginning to make sense at last.

Of course, she could be wrong, but she didn't think she was.

Still, she'd have to wait until they met with Lek to be certain.

She wondered how long the trip would take and decided then to stop worrying about it and enjoy it for what it was—an experience she might never again have.

That thought motivating her, she rode the rest of the silent trip with a smile on her face.

The journey ended far too soon for Jiya's liking.

The same couldn't be said for Ka'nak.

The nearly invisible ship that carried them bumped into a bubble of the same material, which was set into the side of an underwater mountain.

From this close, the entrance looked as if it might only

be a slight cleft in the mountainside, perhaps a slice of the ground having slid away, but once they slipped into the bubble and it sealed behind them, the entrance became much, much more.

The water drained from the bubble, leaving the crew and the Krokans standing there dripping. Ka'nak ripped off his mask and sucked in a deep breath as if he'd been holding his for the hours it had taken to arrive there.

"How the hell can you people stand that all the time?" he asked, his chest a bellows as he struggled to regulate his breathing.

"We've lived here our entire lives," Val explained with a shrug. "It's second nature to us. We don't give it a second thought."

"Remind me to vacation somewhere else," Ka'nak growled. "I thought for sure that giant fish we saw was going to eat us."

Tog laughed. "Don't worry, you're made of meat," he explained, unable to contain his grin. "Those Whels only eat the plants that fill the waters."

"That monstrous thing only eats plants?" Ka'nak asked, eyes still shining.

"Well, on purpose, at least," Tog clarified.

Roe grinned. "Stop antagonizing him, Tog. Lek's waiting for us."

The bubble opened a passageway into the side of the mountain. The Krokans exited and motioned for the crew to follow.

This time the crew was quick to scramble out, desperate for the feel of solid ground beneath their feet.

The rest removed their masks and hung them on hooks

jutting out of the stony wall. Roe led them down a broad tunnel that seemed to go on forever.

Jiya marveled at her surroundings, realizing that she was walking inside a mountain at the bottom of a massive ocean.

The experience was surreal, and she wondered what kind of technology kept the place from collapsing in on itself.

The air smelled fresher there than it had in town. She noted an earthy scent mixed with the water's salty brine, and it was far from unpleasant.

It smelled like a garden after a long night's rain, fresh and enticing. The scent called to her.

Roe and the Krokans seemed to relax once they were inside the underwater mountain. Jiya had a pretty good idea why.

Before, the crew could have run; could have escaped. Now there was nowhere to go that didn't dump them into the ocean.

That's one hell of a security system, she thought.

As they walked, they passed other Krokans, but the similarities ended at the obvious sharing of the race.

These people were bright-eyed, smiling, and happy. They looked well-fed and content, and they were dressed in a variety of clothing that didn't speak of hard times or necessity.

They seemed to dress to flatter their appearance, which caught Jiya and the others off-guard.

There was no sign of the constant war-footing that eclipsed the joy in the city. Here the people were far from the war and its foul effects.

"Different, huh?" Roe asked, seeing Jiya looking about in wonder.

"It is…" she admitted, wanting to say more but not finding the words to adequately explain her feelings.

"This is what it should be back in the city," Roe said, and his grin faltered.

Jiya spied a sparkle of frustration in his eyes before he looked away.

"We're here," he announced after a moment of silence.

The huge tunnel gave way to a giant cavern of a room. Alcoves were carved into the walls like apartments scaling a naturally formed building. Drapes and variously colored sheets hung over the openings to maintain a modicum of privacy, but the majority had been flung open to the world.

Hundreds of people milled about in the various alcoves. Below, a great valley opened up, sporting a miniature city of its own, rooftops and roadways visible from where they perched in the cavern's elevated opening.

"This place goes deeper?" Geroux wondered, barely able to get her tongue to form the question.

"It does," Val confirmed, "although the town center there is as far as most of the residents will ever go."

Roe motioned for the group to veer to the right, where another of the alcoves awaited. He pulled aside the thick leather drapes that sealed it and ushered them inside. The crew stepped into the room to find a meeting hall of some kind, fairly small compared to the mess hall aboard the SD *Reynolds*.

A table was central to the room, and chairs circled it. Roe gestured for the crew to take seats.

Almost as soon as they did, a curtained alcove at the far

end of the room whipped open and an older female walked out. Dressed in soft, silky robes, her long gray hair was pulled back into a tight braid behind her head, making her features look severe and sharp.

The lack of a smile on her face did nothing to disabuse Jiya of the respect this person commanded.

She came over and stood at the opposite end of the table, not bothering to take a seat.

"Lek," Roe began, "these are the off-worlders I spoke of. The ones who came to trade with Jaer Pon. Meet Jiya, Geroux, and Ka'nak."

She nodded at the introductions.

"We appreciate the help with the Orau," Jiya told her, realizing it was probably in their best interests to get on her good side.

Lek remained stone-faced. "That was Roe's doing. If you thank anyone for that, it would be him."

Jiya offered him a nod of appreciation, but Lek wasn't quite done yet.

"Still, I have to wonder why you placed yourself in a situation that required our people to rescue you. Is it not your benefactor's place to provide such assistance?"

"Jaer Pon is not our benefactor," Jiya explained. "He was the person we were directed to when we first arrived, knowing nothing of your world or its people. Had we known there were divisions within the ranks of the Krokans—"

"There are no divisions, I assure you," Lek stated.

Jiya stared at her for a moment, wondering what she meant. Lek seemed to sense her confusion and began again.

"The one you call president, Jaer Pon, is not one of us," she said. "He is not of this world, in fact."

"But he's in control," Geroux said, clearly as confused as Jiya.

"Not all usurpers are native to the planet they usurp," Lek explained.

The look she gave them was almost pitying, as if she thought the crew stupid.

"You mean he took over? A coup?" Jiya asked, seeking clarification.

"In a manner of speaking. Yes, you could call it that," Lek answered. "We, however, prefer to call it an invasion."

"I'm thinking we might need to start taking notes," Geroux whispered to Jiya.

"Further, you and your people are being used to advance Jaer Pon's agenda and control of the rightful people of Krokus 4."

That was something Jiya could grasp without confusion.

"It is not our wish to be pawns in such a game. Can you explain?" she asked, wanting as much information as Lek was willing to provide.

"Your raid upon the Orau on Krokus 1 is a perfect example," she said. "Jaer Pon's greatest political failure in the attempt to maintain control has been his inability to stop the Orau invaders. You assisted him in this matter, thus freeing his resources to deal with the next threat in line."

"Which is you?" Jiya asked, already knowing the answer.

"Us, of course," Lek answered, and Jiya felt her stomach twist at the admission.

"I presume you already know that we were sent here to kill you and your people?" Jiya asked, deciding to lay everything out on the table and see where things fell.

Ka'nak groaned.

"We're not here to kill them," Jiya told the Melowi.

"You sure?" he shot back. "I'm pretty sure that's what President Jaer Pon is expecting in exchange for the supplies and tech we need."

Jiya and Geroux sighed in unison, sinking into their seats.

"Because if we don't—"

Jiya raised a hand, silencing Ka'nak with an impatient wave. "We are *not* here to kill anyone," she stated, meeting Lek's eyes. "Regardless of what Jaer Pon believes we are going to do for him, we are our own people. Our mission is to seek out Kurtherians while establishing safe havens across the galaxy, helping where and when we can, working with the leaders of each planet we visit to better their lives.

"If Jaer Pon is not the rightful ruler of this world, then our deal with him is null and void," Jiya stated with conviction. "We are *no one's* assassins."

"That is good to hear," Lek said, the first smile Jiya had seen spreading across her lips. "If you are here to help the people of Krokus 4 and not harm them then there is much we need to discuss, Jiya."

"I agree," Jiya replied, "I'm only the first officer of the Superdreadnought *Reynolds*. It's not me you need to speak with, but our captain, Reynolds."

"The android?" Lek asked.

Ka'nak chuckled.

"Well, he's not exactly an android," Jiya tried to explain. "He's an artificial intelligence, an AI whose consciousness inhabits both the superdreadnought we came in *and* the android body that came to the planet with us."

"Interesting," Lek said. "And he is in charge of your mission?"

"He is."

Jiya felt bad for a moment about pushing Reynolds in front of the hoverbus, but she knew she was a little out of her depth.

As much as she'd learned about statesmanship and politics from being around her father, this situation paled in comparison. She still hadn't wrapped her head around all the aspects of what was going on and who was who.

The last thing she wanted to do was commit them to the wrong side of the war they'd inadvertently jumped into.

But Reynolds had been right. The Orau were scum and deserved what they'd gotten on Krokus 1. And if Jaer Pon was as bad as they were, then he deserved a swift kick in the ass too.

"Yeah, Reynolds is the person you need to speak to," Jiya reiterated. "I'll put you in touch."

CHAPTER TWENTY-THREE

Maddox stood over the captive, who'd only just begun to wake up when Reynolds arrived.

He stared up at the pair, blurry-eyed and not quite coherent. Reynolds grinned at the bound male, reveling in the moment. He hadn't been able to capture one of the Loranian crew alive to find out what he wanted to know, but after what Maddox told him he'd overheard, this captive was connected to the same group.

That meant the poor bastard was in for a long, long night.

Before he'd fully come to, Reynolds squatted by his face and insisted on asking, "Who are you working for?"

The captive grunted, starting to wave Reynolds away only to realize that his hands were tied. His eyes narrowed, cognizance seeping into his mind as the awareness of his current situation became clear.

"You dare?" he spat back, snarling.

"Oh, I dare," Reynolds answered.

"And then some," Maddox added.

Reynolds glanced over his shoulder the general. Maddox shrugged.

"Just trying to help," the general said.

"Well...don't," Reynolds told him, turning back to the captive.

"I am a servant of the god Phraim-'Eh!" he shouted. "I will not be intimidated by a heathen such as you."

"Well, I guess that's that then," Reynolds agreed, jumping to his feet.

"That's it?" Maddox asked, staring at Reynolds.

"He clearly isn't going to talk, so why waste our time? He's a servant of Phraim-'Eh. Would you talk if you were?"

Maddox stared as if he were unsure if Reynolds was asking him a trick question. He shrugged. "Maybe. I don't know."

"We're done here," Reynolds stated, turning away.

"Seriously?" Maddox and the captive asked at the same time.

Reynolds spun about, slamming the back of his hand into the captive's face.

The blow reverberated through the room and the Krokan rolled back, slamming into the wall. His cheek was bright red, the eye above it already swelling.

"Fuck, no, we're not done, asshole!" Reynolds shouted, coming over and getting in the captive's face again. "Now, unless you want me to violate more than your personal space, I suggest you tell me what the hell I want to know."

Stunned by the blow, the captive's eyes swam in his head.

"How about we start with your name, Mister Servant of Phraim-'Eh. What's your name?"

"Ter Vil," he muttered, a tiny rivulet of blood running from his mouth and down his chin.

"See, that wasn't too bad, was it, Ter?" Reynolds asked, straightening and moving back a step.

Ter groaned and used the wall at his back to sit upright. As his wits returned, his confused stare turned into a glare.

"He's giving you dagger-eyes," Maddox warned, waggling a finger at Ter. "Bad boy."

"He hasn't realized that his boss, Phraim-'Eh, isn't quite the shield against discomfort he originally believed."

"Phraim-'Eh is a god!" Ter shrieked. "He will tear you limb from limb and devour your soul!"

Reynolds grinned inside.

Fucking idiot cultists.

Finding out that Phraim-'Eh was a god wasn't the best of news, but Reynolds knew hyperbole when he heard it.

Their god was a Kurtherian, who thought of themselves as gods but usually weren't so blatant about creating a cult of followers.

"Have you ever heard your god's voice, or does he use a spokesman?" Reynolds asked.

The look on his face gave them their answer.

Reynolds knew the spokesman wasn't a god, only a power-mad piece of shit looking for a legacy to cling to by coming after him or the Federation.

Maybe he was after Bethany Anne or Michael?

Either way, the Kurtherian clan's self-professed pope was biting off more than he could chew.

"What would a god want with little ol' you?" Maddox

asked, pulling a chair over and plopping down in it so he could watch the proceedings.

Reynolds appreciated the general's efforts at disarming the captive.

They worked well as a team, though Reynolds didn't like to think that they were in the process of interrogating a prisoner. Torture was out, but they'd do everything up to that to get answers.

"Well, I *am* pretty charming," Reynolds replied. "I can see how almost any god would want to hang around me. It would up his deity-credit among the other gods, no doubt."

"He will make you pay!" Ter promised, spittle flying as he screamed, "Phraim-'Eh will tear down your Federation and decorate the stars with your ashes."

"Poetic," Maddox noted, nodding. "I'm guessing Phraim-'Eh has a history with your people, Reynolds."

Hearing Ter mention the Kurtherian clan triggered a silent fury in Reynolds. He'd been right.

The Kurtherians had traveled through these worlds, making his mission a valid one. He wasn't chasing ghosts anymore or the distant memories of his old enemy. No, they were still lurking, desperately working against Reynolds and the Federation, hoping to bring it down the same as they'd always done.

They can try, but they've never met anyone like me before.

"It's a shame this Phraim-'Eh fellow, a male I'm presuming, because a female would obviously have been way better at taking you out, feels he needs to hide behind these Loranian twits he keeps sending after you," Maddox pushed.

"Our master is a god!" Ter shouted again. "He needs no

minions to tear your empire down, but he has gathered like-minded souls from all over the universe, the line of his disciples leading all the way back to the start of your existence."

Maddox raised an eyebrow and looked at Reynolds, clearly surprised at how easily the cultist was kept talking.

Reynolds had a momentary concern that Ter was feeding him what Reynolds wanted to hear, but the froth that coated his lips and the signs of legitimate rage permeated the captive's face and posture.

If he thought he had a chance to kill Reynolds and Maddox, he'd do it without hesitation.

Only his bonds were preventing him from trying.

He was a true zealot.

"It's a shame those idiots on that Loranian ship got their asses kicked so easily," Maddox went on. "I'd kind of like to see you take on a god, Reynolds. Maybe we can get old Ter here to give them a call and tell them to come on down for a rematch. Maybe they'll actually put up a fight this time."

"Jora'nal is a messenger of Phraim-'Eh. There is no way you could defeat him," Ter growled. "The *Pillar* stalks you, and you will feel the chill of its presence upon your cowardly spine soon."

Reynolds wanted to laugh but held it in so as not to clue Ter into his stream of transgressions. "Don't make us beat the information out of you!" Reynolds feinted.

"You will get nothing from me!" the captive declared.

Besides, given all the damage his android body had taken, he was afraid he'd blow a gasket if he laughed as hard as he wanted to.

He needed Takal to build him a new body very soon.

That would be the priority once he got back on the superdreadnought, but right now he was getting way too much information from this servant of Phraim-'Eh.

"So, is that a no on the rematch?" Reynolds asked.

Before Ter could respond static crackled through the comm, then Jiya's voice echoed in his head.

"Got someone you really need to meet," she told him.

"Right in the middle of something," he told her, stepping away from the captive so he could talk without being overheard.

"That Jiya?" Maddox asked, coming over to try to listen in.

Reynolds nodded.

"You're going to want to make time, boss," she pressed. "Learned some interesting things about our host *President* Jaer Pon and what's going on around this place. It's eye-opening shit."

"We have a bit of that going on here, too," Reynolds replied, glancing at their captive.

Ter jumped to his feet and shrieked, the sound like a banshee caught in a thresher.

Maddox raced toward him, but Ter charged at the wall and drove the top of his head into the unforgiving stone.

There was a loud *crack*, and Ter Vil slumped to the ground, the top of his shattered head gushing blood and gore.

Maddox dropped to his knees beside the fallen cultist and pressed his hands to the male's neck. After a moment, he shook his head.

"He's gone."

Reynolds nodded. He could have told the general that without touching the body.

He'd heard Ter's heart give way at the same time his skull did.

He sighed and turned his attention back to the comm.

"Well, it appears my schedule just cleared. Where do you want to meet?"

Reynolds met Jiya and the others at an abandoned house on the opposite side of town from where President Jaer Pon had sent the crew to find the Knights of Orau.

"So there aren't really any Knights, huh?" he asked after the crew and Lek and her people had brought him up to speed.

"No, there are not," Lek confirmed. "That was simply a story he told you to align our people with those sickening Orau to gain your sympathy and turn you against us." She sneered. "However, there are certainly many Orau here on this planet."

"Wait, there are?" Jiya asked, bolting upright on the battered couch she'd sat on.

"Indeed," Lek replied. "Jaer Pon himself is one, as are the majority of his council, his followers, his guards, and all those who traveled with him when he first arrived on Krokus 4."

"This gets more and more confusing," Geroux stated.

"You didn't tell me that earlier," Jiya complained.

Lek shrugged. "I felt it best to save such revelations

until we were gathered together, so there would be no need to repeat such an important piece of information."

"You mean we helped an Orau defeat Orau?" Reynolds asked.

"That was exactly what happened," Lek told him, Roe nodding behind her.

"Now I'm confused," Reynolds admitted. "You're going to need to explain this to me."

"We—my people and I—are the original Krokans," Lek started. "Jaer Pon and the others crashed upon our planet, and we fished them from the waters. A long lost tribe of ours has returned home, with a vengeance. Having no knowledge of what they'd become as the Orau, we welcomed them into our homes and lives, believing we were doing what was right and good."

"I still believe that," Roe stated.

Lek nodded. "As do I, but we misjudged Jaer Pon and his ambitions."

Ka'nak glanced at Jiya, expecting the same "I told you so" from Jiya that Reynolds did.

The first officer, however, simply shook her head and continued to listen intently.

Reynolds, proud of her growth, looked back at Lek so she could continue her story.

"It didn't take long before he began to campaign for power," Lek went on. "He whispered honey-scented words into the ears of any who would listen, promising wealth and prosperity our simple people had never before experienced.

"He showed them the tricks of his people's technology. The shield that surrounds this city was his finest moment and the thing that turned our people into believers."

Lek chewed her lower lip as she paused, moved by the memories of what had happened.

"I was young then," she continued. "Well, younger," she clarified with a soft laugh. "But there was much about his offers and his words that didn't ring true to me. So, when Jaer Pon built this city and surrounded it with his dome, we remained in our true home, the place Roe and the others brought your crew to meet me."

"I'd love to see it," Reynolds told her.

From what Jiya and the crew had told him of it, the place was a miracle of architecture that he wanted to see to appreciate.

"And you will, Reynolds, fear not, but first we must undo what you have inadvertently wrought by taking out Jaer Pon's only true enemy: his own people."

"I don't understand what happened between them," Geroux said.

"It's a simple matter of self-importance, I'm afraid," Lek answered. "Jaer Pon believed himself more important than everyone else upon his world, and when the resources of his homeworld had been exhausted and the Orau made to expand to the next, Jaer Pon stole a craft and peopled it with his followers so that he could find a world of his own.

"He fled the Orau, turning his back on his people in hopes of creating his own dynasty, but the past has a way of catching up to those who try to flee it."

Geroux's eyes widened when she realized where Lek was headed.

"Jaer Pon's people followed him here and began their

ritual of raiding the system," Reynolds stated, having already arrived at the logical conclusion.

"Precisely that," Lek confirmed. "Knowledgeable of his people's ways and capabilities, Jaer Pon was able to defend against their advances and keep them from invading the planet wholesale."

"But that can't last forever against a foe whose main tactic is attrition," Jiya added.

Lek nodded. "Unable to replenish the resources necessary to advance and fend off the attacks of his people, Krokus 4 fell into disarray, the entirety of its energy spent upon the meager fleet that now guards the planet," she explained. "A stubborn people, the Orau returned time and time again, settling into bombarding our planet in hopes of wearing the citizenry down to the point that they would eventually collapse or dispose of Jaer Pon, either of which would have had the same effect. Without another means of protecting ourselves, the Orau would have installed another leader. We were to remain trapped, no matter which way the war turned.

"Without the knowledge of the shield, which only Jaer Pon truly understands, the city would be washed away, and the Orau would claim what is left of the planet's resources."

"What about the military?" Reynolds asked. "If we challenge Jaer Pon, will they rise against us?"

"Unlikely," Lek replied.

"Colonel Raf is a pragmatist," Roe explained. "He will follow the will of the people, doing what is best for them, not the whims of a tyrannical leader."

"Will you take the president's place, when all is said and done?" Geroux asked.

Reynolds smiled. It was a smart question.

Lek shook her head. "I have no interest in politics. I'm too old for all that anyway. I would leave the effort to younger minds and cooler heads, but I would happily advise those who come after Jaer Pon. I will serve our people to the best of my ability."

"We would approach Vice President Shal Ura," Roe stated. "She sees what's happening to her adopted world and views things differently than Jaer Pon. She is no longer an Orau so much as she is a Krokan now, whatever her original status."

"So you would hand the planet back to the same people in charge of it now?" Reynolds asked.

"We would hand it back to the people," Lek corrected. "To those who would see it prosper, safe from those who would bring it down while simultaneously exploiting our people and resources."

Reynolds nodded his reply, giving himself a moment to collect his thoughts.

He was impressed with Lek, and although he'd made a mistake siding with Jaer Pon when they'd first arrived, he understood that his ignorance had played a role in that decision.

Along with the crew, they'd seen their way through it all, learning about the world and its people and determining what the true story was just as they had in the missions before. The Orau on Krokus 1 needed to be destroyed, and they had been. Now the Orau on Krokus 4 were going to get their turn in the gunsights.

He was proud of his crew.

Despite his earlier mistakes, it wasn't too late to correct them and set things right.

Besides, much of what they'd done was something that needed to be done anyway. Now, there was really only one last problem to address before he and the crew could look to the stars again and chase down the Kurtherians and their minions that had been shadowing them the entire time.

"I have an idea how to fix our mutual problem," Reynolds announced. "If you're interested, that is."

Roe grinned, and Lek waited for the explanation.

"Time to kick one last Orau ass!" Jiya chimed in.

"Count me in on that," Ka'nak offered.

Reynolds smiled. "Okay, folks, looks like we've a planet to take back."

"We're going to need a head, though," Geroux said, reminding them of the president's expectations.

Reynolds grimaced. "I'd forgotten about that."

"Jaer Pon wants my head?" Lek asked.

Reynolds paused for a moment before nodding.

Lek sat there a moment quietly, then a soft grin broke across her cheeks.

"So be it," she said. "My head he shall have."

CHAPTER TWENTY-FOUR

Jiya and the crew slipped away from the meeting with Lek and the other Krokans unseen by the presidential guard or anyone who might report their whereabouts.

She gingerly carried the thick bag that contained the grisly prize Jaer Pon had requested. She hated the way it felt in her hands and she wanted to pass it off, but every time she thought to do that she felt Reynolds' judging eyes on her.

She knew she was imagining it every time, but she couldn't help but feel this was a burden she needed to carry as the *Reynolds'* first officer. *It* wasn't something she could pawn off on Geroux or any of the others.

Well, except Ka'nak, but he'd enjoy the duty too much.

He'd probably make friends with the bloody, severed head.

Jiya shuddered at the thought.

Reynolds had reached out to the compound a short while ago and Sergeant Gib met them outside. He smiled at the crew, nodding at Ka'nak and Geroux, then spotted the moist sack Jiya carried.

His face paled, but to his credit, he didn't turn away.

He simply spun on his heel and waved the crew after him.

They made their way through the halls of the smaller compound, the one they'd met Jaer Pon in previously. Jiya was surprised at how quiet the place was compared to the other.

No servants or workers were roaming the halls. No one was actually, except for the occasional guard who stared cold-eyed at the crew as they passed.

It made sense, she thought. Who wants witnesses to receiving the hacked-off head of a political opponent?

Regardless of the clout earned from taking Lek out, parading her head around likely wouldn't endear Jaer Pon to the people he'd subjugated upon his arrival.

He'd won their support through guile and deceit rather than outright brutality. To make a public spectacle of Lek's defeat would work against him even now, so it made sense to keep it quiet, given the manner in which it was obtained.

No leader who took the heads of their people reigned for long.

While those morbid thoughts played through her head, Sergeant Gib led them back to the makeshift throne room they'd visited the last time. He ushered them inside, and Jiya was glad to see the room looked much the same as it had before.

The only difference was that there were far fewer guards stationed within the room.

As a matter of fact, there were hardly any at all.

Vice President Shal Ura was there, and Flor stood at her side. President Jaer Pon was present, too, as was Minister To Gul, but Jiya counted only five guards positioned around the small dais at the front of the room.

"Welcome! Welcome!" Jaer Pon cried out as they entered. "Please, come in and join us," he said, waving at the crew.

Sergeant Gib nudged the crew forward, staying behind to close the doors.

"I guess all it takes is a little head to make a male happy," Jiya quipped, shaking the bag in her hand.

Geroux looked at her in disgust.

"Tactical would be proud," Reynolds muttered, shaking his head. "Too soon, probably."

The crew made their way to the dais and stopped before the stairs.

Jaer Pon met them with a huge smile. Shal Ura looked ready to be sick, her gaze subconsciously shifting between the crew and the bag Jiya carried.

The vice president knew what it contained.

"Your mission was a success, I take it?" Jaer Pon asked, rising from his chair and coming down the steps to meet them face to face. His gaze scanned the crew exuberantly.

"It was," Reynolds replied, holding out his hand for Jiya to pass him the bag.

"Excellent," he cooed, rubbing his hands together as Jiya gave Reynolds the sack containing the head.

The AI passed it to the president, who undid the ties and took a surreptitious look inside, not allowing anyone else to get a clear view of what was in there.

A great smile lit his face a moment later, and he let out a

long, satisfied sigh. He re-tied the bag, keeping its contents from prying eyes, and handed it to Minister To Gul, who'd come over to stand at his side while he inspected the package.

"You've done well, Reynolds," Jaer Pon told him, clapping the android on the shoulder. "You have the appreciation of the people of Krokus 4, my friends."

He spun and practically danced up the steps to reclaim his seat on the dais.

"We must celebrate this great victory," he called. "Minister To Gul, take that horrid remnant away and rally the servants. Today we feast!"

The minister shuffled off with Jaer Pon's prize, and Jiya watched him go, half-expecting an army of determined soldiers to burst through the door and try to kill them.

But nothing happened.

The old male swung the doors wide and marched through, letting Sergeant Gib close them after he was gone.

No one jumped out at them, tried to assassinate them, or even screamed, "Boo!"

Jiya didn't know whether to be disappointed or happy that she had been so wrong.

Lek had led them to believe that President Jaer Pon would immediately set his guards upon the crew once they dropped off proof that they'd killed her.

She'd been so certain that she had warned them several times, as had Roe. The fact that there were but five guards not counting Sergeant Gib in the room made her question Lek's story now.

"This is a great time for the Krokan people," Jaer Pon went on. "We are rid of the Orau, and we have great friends who will help us to defend our planet from similar invaders in the future."

Is that why he's waiting? Jiya wondered. *He wants the technology first?*

But that didn't make sense. While the Orau and Krokans weren't overly sophisticated technology-wise, they had more than sufficient ability to crack open Reynolds' skull and take what they needed from the AI trapped in the android's body.

Lek and Roe had made that clear too.

What were they waiting for?

Jiya found herself glancing around the room as the president went on, listing the plans he had for their celebration, who he would invite, what they would eat, and how long into the week the celebratory parties would last.

She glanced at Reynolds, who stared back at her with a blank expression. She could read the look in his eyes, though.

It was the exact same as the one in hers.

What the absolute fuck?

What's going on? she asked over her implanted communicator link.

I have no idea, Reynolds admitted. *Maybe we judged him wrong?*

He's definitely happy that Lek is dead, but I'm not seeing the murderous rage to get rid of all the witnesses and accomplices she and Roe predicted, Jiya said.

Well, we are *dealing with people and cultures we know nothing about,* Reynolds suggested. *Maybe we wait and see?*

Jiya hated waiting.

"Mister President," she asked, raising her hand, "did you want the defense ring technology?"

Jaer Pon waved the question off. "Later, my friends. After we celebrate. This is a day of joy," he said. "I would have us enjoy our victory. All talks of politics and negotiations can wait."

Jiya directed a subtle shrug Reynolds' way. She'd pushed, and Jaer Pon had blown off the opportunity to get what she'd thought he wanted.

And still, no guards broke down the door or armies spilled into the room to try to kill or capture the crew.

Unsure what to do, the crew stood there stupidly, waiting for the president.

All the while, he chatted excitedly with the vice president, who still looked sullen and disinterested, and then with Flor about the feast plans,. At last, as if he'd only just realized the crew was still standing there, he turned his attention back to them.

"Oh, please, no more standing around. You must be exhausted after all you've done," he started. "Let Flor show you to your quarters so you can rest. The celebrations will begin at nightfall, so conserve your energy until then. The whole of Krokus 4 will want to congratulate you and show their appreciation." He grinned broadly. "It will, no doubt, be even more exhausting than the missions you have completed," he finished with a chuckle, waving the crew on before going back to speaking with Shal Ura.

Flor smiled and motioned toward the doors.

"This way, please," she told them. "I'll show you to your quarters,

Reynolds, caught off guard by the strange results of

their meeting with Jaer Pon, shrugged and motioned for the crew to follow Flor to their guest chambers.

She opened the doors to show the crew out, and Jiya wondered if maybe things were exactly what they appeared to be for once.

No subterfuge, no bullshit.

Just good old-fashioned honesty, where people did what they said and followed through on their promises.

That was when Reynolds was shot dead in the chest.

Geroux screamed when Reynolds stumbled back, a charred hole blasted in the middle of his chest where a normal creature's heart might be. Wisps of smoke spilled from the wound.

Sergeant Gib stood there with a twisted smile on his face and his gun barrel smoldering.

As badly as Jiya wanted to be pissed about the attack—scared, worried, whatever—she found herself relieved to have the ambush come at last.

She was glad, too, that it had been the AI who'd taken the first shot and not one of the others in the crew.

"Motherfucker!" Reynolds cursed, prodding the hole in his android body.

The AI was pissed.

Dozens of presidential guards crowded the doorway, aiming their weapons into the room.

Flor shrieked and dove aside.

"Maddox!" Jiya screamed.

"On it." The general's voice came from less than two meters away.

Maddox appeared in his armor out of nowhere behind the crowd of guards and opened up with his pistol, blasting them in the back with measured, careful shots.

San Roche and L'Eliana appeared right beside him and did the same, the three of them mowing down the guards with murderous precision.

The soldiers spun to face the surprise attack and were immediately plowed into by Reynolds and Ka'nak.

While the crew in the throne room were unarmed, it was a mistake to think they were incapable of dishing out damage.

Hurt as he was, Reynolds flung guards around as if they were motes of dust. Guards screamed and howled as he tore through them while the three crewmembers shot them down from the other side.

Ka'nak relished the opportunity to fight, ripping the guards apart as he stood alongside Reynolds.

Jiya and Geroux stepped away from the carnage as bodies flew, limbs flailing.

"We've got more flooding in the front entrance," Maddox warned from the hallway, his voice carrying over the comm and through the room at the same time.

"Now, Geroux," Jiya told her friend.

The young tech didn't bother to respond, her fingers flying over the keypad of her wrist computer. Not more than a second later the power in the small compound flickered and died, drowning the room in darkness.

Darkness the crew could see in perfectly, thanks to Takal's brilliant technique of shrinking the cumbersome night-vision goggles so they could be used as permanent contacts inserted in the eyes of the crew.

Of course, the process hurt like hell, Jiya recalled, but the results were worth every second of it.

"Get that piece of shit," Reynolds shouted to her and Jiya grinned.

"On it," she replied, racing toward the dais at the far end of the room.

Jaer Pon, a master of survival, had already abandoned his chair and fled toward the alcove at the back where he'd pulled the body of the supposed Knight from earlier.

Jiya knew there was a door there, Roe having told her of it.

Vice President Shal Ura screamed and dove for cover in the darkness as the five guards on the dais made their way down the steps as carefully as they could in the absolute blackness of the room.

Jiya figured they'd expected to stand their ground and be close-in protection for the president should something go wrong with the ambush, but they hadn't expected the sudden dearth of lights.

That made them easy targets for Jiya and Geroux.

Jiya stepped up to the first of the guards and shot him in the head, ducking away to make herself harder to hit since she'd just announced her position.

Geroux helped with that.

The young tech crouched and blasted another of the guards, strafing her fire across to take out a third. With Shal Ura huddled face-down on the floor, Geroux didn't have to worry about accidentally hitting her.

Jiya killed the last two guards, shooting one, then

swiveling to get the next one. It took a second shot to kill the last of them, but it had been as satisfying as the first.

Backstabbing assholes!

She hurtled up the dais steps after Jaer Pon.

As she did, she heard the shout of furious warriors and the crash of flesh against flesh.

She cast a quick glance over her shoulder as she ran and spied Lek's people storming the hallway, overtaking the squad of presidential guards that had rushed in to back up the first group.

And then she was through the covered alcove and hard on the heels of the president, the door to his secret hallway hanging wide open.

While she'd had a few minutes of concern when he'd acted far different than she'd expected, she was now fully invested in Lek's intel.

She knew exactly where the hidden passage went and where it came out, so she ran through it without worry, recalling that there was only one secretive alcove he might hide in before it led into the night.

Her magnified vision had made it clear the narrow cubby was empty before she'd approached, so she passed it, flying down the hall after the president.

She could hear his slapping footsteps and his huffed breaths ahead of her. A flicker of motion told her she was closing in on him. He was going to make it to the exit before she reached him, though.

Jiya cursed and doubled down, pushing harder to catch him.

There was no way in hell she was going to let him get away.

She spotted the open door of the tunnel just ahead, Jaer Pon scrambling through it, desperately trying to stay ahead of her. Jiya was almost on top of him.

She raised her weapon and kept running, bursting through the door right behind him.

He shrieked when he ran into a wall of people who'd come out of nowhere.

Brilliant lights instantly illuminated the area and Jiya blinked away the brightness, grateful that Takal's tech had a failsafe, adjusting to even the most sudden or extreme changes in lighting.

She staggered to a halt as Lek grinned at her.

Her people grabbed Jaer Pon, holding him firmly with rough and firm hands.

A little surprised to see her, Jiya looked from the captive president to Lek.

"I thought all of your people were backing up my crew," Jiya said.

"And miss out on seeing Jaer Pon's face when he found out I was alive and well?" she asked, chuckling. "I think not, young lady."

Jaer Pon didn't even bother to squirm. He stared at Lek, wide-eyed and terrified.

"Maybe he thinks he's seeing a ghost," Jiya suggested.

"Well, your inventor's replica android head had me thinking that maybe I *had* lost mine somewhere along the way," Lek chuckled. "I hadn't expected it to look quite so…real."

"Takal has his talents," Jiya said.

"That he does," Lek agreed.

Reynolds stumbled out of the tunnel entrance right

then. Vice President Shal Ura clung to his arm, and the rest of the crew stood there grinning from ear to ear. Roe and his troops stood at their backs, happy to see Jaer Pon in the arms of their companions.

"*Now* it's a party!" Reynolds shouted.

CHAPTER TWENTY-FIVE

Reynolds stood before the captive Jaer Pon, wagging a finger at him.

"I have to say, I'm not appreciating Sergeant Gib blasting a hole in the only good body I have right now," he said.

"You've still got the Jonny-Taxi one," Ka'nak suggested.

"And how you missed being shot when you went through the door first is a mystery to me," Reynolds stated, glaring at the Melowi.

Ka'nak barked a laugh, and Reynolds turned his attention back to Jaer Pon.

"You had me there for a minute," Reynolds admitted. "I was just about to switch sides again and throw my lot back in with you, Mister Prez, but you went and fucked it all up."

Jaer Pon sneered, but it didn't carry much of a threat since he was trussed up like a turkey ready to go into the oven.

"Don't worry, Reynolds," Lek told him, "He'll pay for his transgressions. You can be certain of that."

"Of that, I have no doubt, Lek," Reynolds replied. "It's just that it's sometimes more satisfying when you get to shoot a betrayer in the face in the heat of combat."

"So it's not just me that feels that way?" Ka'nak asked.

"What's going to happen now?" Geroux asked, fiddling with her wrist computer.

Lek held a hand out to Shal Ura. The vice president took it and Lek passed her over to Roe, the two locking hands.

"We'll let the people decide who rules them from now on, but we have a pair of candidates from both sides of the people to keep things in order until that happens. It'll be a solid move toward cooperation."

Roe grinned at Shal Ura, who smiled right back. While Jiya saw the mutual respect between the pair, she wondered if her imagination was playing tricks on her since she saw a little bit more than mutual professional admiration flash between them when their eyes locked.

She didn't have time to think about it further.

"And the rest of the Orau here on the planet?" Reynolds asked. "They'll fall in line with this?" He gestured to the temporary leaders.

Lek nodded. "They will since they feel they are Krokans anyway. Colonel Raf has already informed the fleet of the change in leadership and the military has pledged their loyalty to the new government of the people."

"What will you do with him?" Geroux asked, pointing to Jaer Pon, who was doing his best to slink into the background noise.

"We'll imprison him for a time, I think. At least until the government is settled," Roe answered, Shal Ura nodding her agreement with the decision. "After that, we'll leave it to the people to decide, same as their method of governance."

"That seems rather...lenient," Jiya said.

Roe shrugged. "Don't underestimate the will of the people when it comes to revenge," he said with a laugh. "Once news gets out that he ordered Lek's head brought to him as proof of her death and celebrated its delivery, however fake it might have been, I suspect any goodwill he might have earned over the years will be erased quite effectively."

"He will be punished, of that, you can be certain," Shal Ura stated. "He has long tied the hands of the people with his schemes to keep us divided, but we will stand for it no longer."

"Then it seems we only have a couple pieces of business left to us here on Krokus 4," Reynolds announced, glancing at Lek.

"Indeed," she said, offering him a pleasant smile. "You have fulfilled your end of the bargain you struck with Jaer Pon and then some. We would gladly call you friend to the people of Krokus 4 and provide you with a safe haven in your time of need, supplies as necessary when you visit our planet, and the schematics of the great water purification system as you were promised."

Lek cleared her throat and looked down at Jaer Pon.

"Of course, we'll need to pry the latter out of his head first, but I assure you we will send them your way the moment they are available. You have our word."

Reynolds chuckled and gave her a shallow bow of appreciation.

"We look forward to it," he replied. "And in return, we offer the means not only for your people to build a defense ring around your planet to protect against further Orau invasion or anyone else who might happen along but also the means to create your own supply of food safely and easily without the need for large tracts of land or even soil."

Lek's eyebrow rose in surprise. "This is possible?"

"It is indeed," Reynolds assured. "You'll no doubt need to fine-tune the devices to your people's dietary needs, and it will take some effort to get the system up and running, as we're learning ourselves, but in no time at all, you'll be able to eat something that doesn't involve fish."

A cheer rose from the crowd who had heard the last statements and Jiya laughed, watching the Krokans enjoying the moment.

"Will you stay with us to celebrate?" Roe asked. "We promise not to ambush you during the festivities like the previous administration," he added with a chuckle.

"Where's the fun in that?" Ka'nak asked, a half-smile pulling at his face.

Reynolds grinned. "I think we can stick around and relax for a little while," he told Roe. "We've got work to do on Krokus 1, and it'll take time to get your planet up to speed and ready for the new technologies."

"Vacation at last!" Maddox exclaimed, pumping his arm.

Jiya patted the general on the shoulder. "Honestly, with all the excitement, I'm looking forward to curling up in my tiny bunk and sleeping for a week or two after all this."

"And miss out on the celebration?" Roe asked.

"Will there be coffee?" Jiya fired back. "I could really use some go-juice if I'm expected to stay awake."

"I'm sure we can find you some," Shal Ura assured her.

"Then I'm ready to party," Jiya said with a laugh. "Let's do this!"

EPILOGUE

Despite Jiya's desire to fall asleep and not wake up until the next decade, the crew spent the next several weeks on Krokus 4.

Between the celebration, the efforts to establish a new government, and the exchange of information, Jiya had begun to believe they might never leave the planet.

There were tearful and heartfelt farewells by the time they packed up to leave on both the side of the crew and the people of Krokus 4.

But it wasn't all good news.

While Takal worked on a new android body for Reynolds, one that would support the entirety of his AI essence, the captain was stuck in the Jonny-Taxi body he'd started out in.

He hated every minute of it.

By the time they'd left the planet and made their way back to Krokus 1, he was itching to Gate across the galaxy and drag every Kurtherian out of the dark just so he could kick their asses and make himself feel better about being trapped in that horrible body.

The upside during that time was that was the people of Krokus 1 were quick studies, so it wasn't long before they had the agroprinters up and running and abundantly supplying their people with fresh food and drinks.

It had been so long since they'd had anything but the scraps tossed aside by the invading Orau that the crew had to teach them about moderation and when to say no.

The majority of the planet's population was sick the first week or so, but they adapted and overcame, curtailing their zeal.

While the planet was still largely barren and desiccated thanks to the Orau invasion, the people of Krokus 1 decided they wanted to remain.

Jiya thought that was a bold move.

Shal Ura and Roe, both having decided to forego titles until a true election had been held to validate their positions, promised to assist the people of Krokus 1 and sent Colonel Raf and a legion of his soldiers to the planet to assist.

Their mission was to build stronger and better structures for the people to live and work in, with the hopes of the new infrastructure that would last until the people could get on their feet and do more for themselves.

No matter what, it was better than the ramshackle huts and thrown-together buildings the Orau had erected.

Takal and Geroux had pitched in and updated the network systems to facilitate better contact between the two worlds, as well as with the SD *Reynolds*. By the time they were done, the place was modern and rivaled the sophistication of Krokus 4.

That wasn't saying much, Jiya thought, *but it was a far cry from where they'd started just a few weeks earlier.*

They were free.

As far as Jiya was concerned, everything else was gravy.

Reynolds agreed, promising to swing back through the system to check on the Krokans at the next available opportunity.

After all their work, the crew was ready to head back into space.

On the bridge of the *Reynolds*, Jiya relaxed in the captain's chair, letting Asya take a break.

Reynolds paced in front of the viewscreen, his Jonny-Taxi body stumping about like it needed a good oiling. Star maps flashed across the screen so quickly that Jiya had stopped trying to keep up with the AI's mad desire to plot a new course.

After what seemed an eternity, a map came up on the screen and remained there.

"This our next adventure?" Jiya asked, yawning. She still needed that nap.

"I'm not sure," Reynolds replied, not bothering to turn around. "I've been wracking my brain and trying to track down any and all information on this Phraim-'Eh spokesperson and his cult, but there is little to be found." He sighed.

"There are traces of the cult on Loran, and it's clear these guys have been following us since I picked up you and your people from Lariest. I'm just not understanding how all the pieces of the puzzle fit together."

"Before he killed himself, the cultist implied his master and this Phraim-'Eh person had been tracking Reynolds since long before we met him," Maddox added.

"He made his intentions clear, too," Reynolds went on. "We're not going to be rid of this Loranian cruiser until we blow it out of space, and even that might not be enough. There's more to this than some personal vendetta if the cultist is to be believed."

"But you weren't able to get a location out of the guy?" Jiya asked.

Reynolds shook his head. "He was a fanatic. I think when he realized he'd inadvertently told us almost everything he knew that he snapped, deciding to kill himself before he had to face his master and his god."

"Hell of a way to go," Maddox muttered.

"Where does that leave us?" Jiya wondered.

"Well, it's not just a Loranian thing," Reynolds explained. "There were people of a number of different races involved in the plot to kill us, and they seem to be Kurtherian-backed."

"So we keep doing what we're doing then, following the breadcrumbs from system to system until we find the bastards?" Jiya asked.

"Pretty much," Reynolds replied, "but we might try something a little different this time around. I've isolated the names of the species of the male in charge of the shuttle crew on Krokus 1."

"The melted-cheese-faced one?" Maddox asked.

"That's the one," Reynolds said. "He's a Muultu from the planet Muultar in the Quadrain system not too far from here," the AI reported, examining the data on the screen.

"The planet is the polar opposite of Krokus 4. Muultar has almost *no* water. It's a bleak and barren place, and the system has three suns. Because of its rotation between all three of them, the place never sees anything resembling night. They're continuously being cooked by one or another of the suns."

"That explains why they look like that." Maddox gestured to the screen, where Reynolds had brought up an image of the Muultu.

"Makes me wonder if I turned the oven off before we left," Tactical mumbled.

"You thinking we might find more about this Phraim-'Eh cult leader there?" Jiya asked.

Reynolds shrugged. "Worth a shot, seeing as how we lost the Loranian cruiser after that last battle. They vanished to lick their wounds."

"They'll be back," Maddox assured the AI. "Those bastards have an agenda, and they've been damn persistent so far. No reason to think they're going to suddenly stop, especially since they survived the ESD. They'll come back better and stronger."

"I'm counting on it," Reynolds replied. "But until then, we can't just sit around waiting and wondering what they're up to and when they'll show up again. Besides, if we can track down this cult the Kurtherians are using as a front against us, maybe we can find out who this Phraim-'Eh figurehead *really* is and give him a nice 'hello, how do you do.'"

"With the ESD, preferably," Tactical added. "Followed by a side of railgun."

"Maybe we can get some intel on this Jora'nal character

who's supposed to be captaining the Loranian cruiser while we're at it," Maddox said.

Reynolds stared at the screen in silence for a moment longer, then muttered something Jiya didn't catch. He then stumped over to one of the open console seats and flopped down.

As much as he complained about the newer android body he'd been stuffed into, Jiya knew it was light years ahead of the Jonny-Taxi one they'd commandeered back on Lariest.

Being forced back into that tin can was grating on the AI's mood. Jiya figured it was more than just a little frustration or depression at having to downgrade, however temporary.

Geroux had said the body couldn't contain the entirety of what made up the AI's consciousness, and that every moment he spent in it, more of him degraded. He feared he'd lose something vital in the meantime, the system robbing him of his full potential and knowledge.

The bridge door hissed open, drawing Jiya from her thoughts and disturbing the sullen silence that had settled over the bridge while they'd each retreated to their own thoughts.

Geroux came in grinning, San Roche and L'Eliana at her side. The two Telluride looked the happiest Jiya had seen them since they'd boarded the superdreadnought.

"Should we be nervous?" Jiya asked, seeing the sly looks they passed between themselves.

She wondered what they were up to.

"Only if amazing and awesome things scare you," the young tech fired back.

"A little," Jiya admitted jokingly.

Geroux giggled. "Well, you're going to have to put up with this one for the foreseeable future, I'm afraid. No way around it."

Before Jiya could ask what the hell her friend was prattling on about, there was a thump of heavy steps and Takal came into the room with a boxy device in his hands. At his heels was a person Jiya had never seen before.

By instinct, heart racing, she leapt to her feet and grabbed her pistol, half-drawing it before Takal's bright-faced amusement stopped her. She hesitated for a moment, took in the scene, and holstered her gun again.

"Impressive, isn't he?" Takal asked, unable to stop grinning, his rosy cheeks gleaming under the bridge lights. He looked like a child in a toy shop.

"What is that?" Maddox said, staring at him. "Is that a…"

Jiya stared closer at Takal's companion, and that was when she realized it wasn't a male at all.

It was an android.

Reynolds jumped up and ran over to stand face to face with it. Jonny-Taxi eyes wide, he ogled the synthetic creation that had been crafted to look like the humans from the world Reynolds came from.

Quite realistically, Jiya had to admit if her video knowledge was anything to go by.

"I figured you've spent enough time clumping around in that junky body you're currently in, Reynolds," Takal remarked. "Enough moping. Let's get you upgraded."

Reynolds stared at the replacement body enthralled, examining it from every angle.

Jiya laughed, but she could see why Reynolds was so entranced. She marveled at the advancement of the android form compared to the last two bodies Reynolds had inhabited.

This one was sleek, and it was covered in a faux-flesh that made it look realistic even beyond first glance. She suspected it could pass for a living being almost everywhere as long as no one looked too closely.

The body was built sturdy, yet sleek and tall, with bright eyes and dark hair, and it wore the uniform Takal had placed on it perfectly.

He looked every bit the officer Reynolds pictured himself as, Jiya realized.

Reynolds straightened after a moment of looking at the new body and grinned as broadly as his battered Jonny-Taxi face could manage. He spun around to face the crew with a flourish.

"Why are all of you standing around gawking?" he shouted. "We've got a mission to get to. Find your stations."

Still laughing, Jiya straightened and saluted the AI. "Sir, yes, sir."

"Set a course for Muultar. Let's see if we can find these nut-swinging minions of Phraim-'Eh before they come back and catch us with our pants down around our ankles," he ordered.

Reynolds grabbed the inventor by the arm and dragged him toward the bridge door.

"Come on, Takal," he said excitedly. "What do you say we take this new body for a test drive?"

The pair left the bridge in a rush and Jiya grinned, then had Helm set the course Reynolds had ordered.

She wasn't going to get that nap after all, but that was okay.

With enough coffee in her system, she was ready for the next adventure.

"Set course for Muultar, Ensign Ria. We'll engage when Reynolds gives the command. XO, verify that repairs are complete and weapons systems have been restored to one hundred percent. And Ensign, next time don't jump us into the middle of someone else's war."

"I'll do my best, sir," Ria replied, "but no promises."

The End

If you liked this book, please leave a review. This is a new series, so the only way I can decide whether to commit more time to it is by getting feedback from you, the readers. Your opinion matters to me. Continue or not? I have only so much time to craft new stories. Help me invest that time wisely. Plus, reviews buoy my spirits and stoke the fires of creativity.

Don't stop now! Keep turning the pages as Craig talks about his thoughts on this book and the overall project called the Age of Expansion.

AUTHOR NOTES - CRAIG MARTELLE

WRITTEN DECEMBER 11, 2018

Thank you for reading this book and you're still reading! Oorah, hard chargers. I really hope you liked this story.

December 11th – yes, I'm writing these the morning of publication. I almost missed them, but Steve kept me on the straight and narrow. It's 3:30 AM and of course it's dark, but where I live, 150 miles from the Arctic Circle, it'll be dark for about 20 hours today. The sun will rise in the south, cruise along the southern horizon for a few hours and then set in the south. It's a completely different world up here.

It has gotten cold, but nothing like the norm, until later this week when we'll be hitting minus twenty Fahrenheit.

It's about zero right now. And Phyllis the Arctic Dog just got up. I better take her for her walk and then I'll be back. I doubt you'll miss me, but a half mile in the chill should sharpen my brain. See you in about twenty minutes.

It's clear right now, which usually means extreme cold, but the benefit is that ofttimes the aurora is out and dancing across the sky. It wasn't out this morning, but it was blazing yesterday. The clouds are starting to roll in as it is supposed to snow. Then tomorrow, back to clear and really cold.

Superdreadnought 3 took us a while and was difficult to write. Tim and I both had a conference in between. We went to Vegas to spend quality time with 700 other self-published authors. But then Tim got sick. I couldn't breathe. We jammed the words, but they were hard words. It took us a while in reviewing them and getting them right. The Just In Time readers, and especially my insider team of Micky, Kelly, Jim, and now John helped us over the finish line.

The end result is a pretty good product that I am proud to have attached to my name (well, my military science fiction pen name, that is).

Talking about mil sci-fi (okay, I will always talk mil sci-fi, even without a segue), Metal Legion 1 – Scorpion's Fury launches in six days. That is one of the best books I've ever been a part of. The story rocks. We added a dozen military science fiction readers to ensure accuracy. The feedback was overwhelmingly positive. I am stoked to see that series hit the street. We already have the first three books done! I held them so I could launch the a new book in the series every two weeks, starting with the first one on December

17th. We'll have at least four books and probably five delivered at that frequency and these are great stories. I am stoked for you to get them.

So many new books coming out. I don't know where to start.

- Monster Case Files 1 (with Kathryn Hearst) is in good shape, too, and has gotten two thumbs up from my insider team. Monster Case Files 2 is getting its initial outline. Monster Case Files is a young adult cozy mystery series. Cozy mysteries are stories where the perp is one of the people you meet during the story. There are no surprise criminals. It is someone you know, but how and most importantly why are the things to be solved. The first story has been beta read and they were over the moon with the book. We'll launch these in March and like Metal Legion, every two weeks, like clockwork, you'll get a new story. They'll be shorter at about 30k words, but they'll be cheaper, too, with full price of only $2.99. They'll have some internal artwork as well. - End Days 1, Blue Apocalypse (with Brian King) is finished and ready to go to the editor. We'll publish this one probably in January. The cover is ordered and will be ready by New Year's. End Days 2 has the first few words written. This is a post-apocalyptic adventure. Can one man get to his son on the other side of the country? Strange happenings are causing chaos. - Mystically Engineered 1 - Dragon Invasion (with Valerie Emerson) is done and in the can, waiting for ME2 to be finished so we can launch them fairly close together. ME2 has 10k words already. Dragons in space. I don't think I need to say much more about this one, but it is an exciting adventure. - Metamorphosis Alpha 3 (with James M. Ward) is over half way done. I took a month to get my latest chapter done. Sorry Jim. I think we can still have it done in time for GaryCon. I better order the cover:)

So much going on and so little time. That's why I forgot these notes. I promise to do better, Steve! But here we are. I'm trying to wrap a few things before we hit the road. My son married into Australia so now we go down under each year to see him and his family. I thank you again, good readers, for staying on board and reading the stories that can take you away for a few hours. Escape with us to a different place.

Peace fellow humans.

Craig Martelle's other books (listed by series)

For a complete list of books from Craig, please see
www.craigmartelle.com

Terry Henry Walton Chronicles (co-written with Michael Anderle) – a post-apocalyptic paranormal adventure

Gateway to the Universe (co-written with Justin Sloan & Michael Anderle) – this book transitions the characters from the Terry Henry Walton Chronicles to The Bad Company

The Bad Company (co-written with Michael Anderle) – a military science fiction space opera

End Times Alaska (also available in audio) – a Permuted Press publication – a post-apocalyptic survivalist adventure

The Free Trader – a Young Adult Science Fiction Action Adventure

Cygnus Space Opera – A Young Adult Space Opera (set in the Free Trader universe)

Darklanding (co-written with Scott Moon) – a Space Western

Rick Banik – Spy & Terrorism Action Adventure

Become a Successful Indie Author – a non-fiction work

Enemy of my Enemy (co-written with Tim Marquitz) – a galactic alien military space opera

Superdreadnought (co-written with Tim Marquitz) – a military space opera

BOOKS BY MICHAEL ANDERLE

For a complete list of books by Michael Anderle, please visit:

www.lmbpn.com/ma-books/

All LMBPN Audiobooks are Available at Audible.com and iTunes

To see all LMBPN audiobooks, including those written by
Michael Anderle please visit:

www.lmbpn.com/audible

Made in the USA
Columbia, SC
26 May 2024